FOUL PLAY

BOOKS BY STUART WOODS

FICTION

Foul Play*

Class Act*

Double Jeopardy*

Hush-Hush*

Shakeup*

Choppy Water*

Hit List*

Treason*

Stealth*

Contraband*

Wild Card*

A Delicate Touch*

Desperate Measures*

Turbulence*

Shoot First*

Unbound*

Quick & Dirty*

Indecent Exposure*

Fast & Loose*

Below the Belt*

Sex, Lies & Serious Money*

Dishonorable Intentions*

Family Jewels*

Scandalous Behavior*

Foreign Affairs*

Naked Greed*

Hot Pursuit*

Insatiable Appetites*

Paris Match*

Cut and Thrust*

Carnal Curiosity*

Standup Guy*

Doing Hard Time*

Unintended Consequences*

Collateral Damage*

Severe Clear*

Unnatural Acts*

D.C. Dead*

Son of Stone*

Bel-Air Dead*

Strategic Moves*

Santa Fe Edge†

Lucid Intervals*

Kisser*

Hothouse Orchid‡

Loitering with Intent*

Mounting Fears§

Hot Mahogany*

Santa Fe Dead†

Beverly Hills Dead

Shoot Him If He Runs*

Fresh Disasters*

Short Straw†

Dark Harbor*

Iron Orchid‡

Two Dollar Bill*

The Prince of Beverly Hills

Reckless Abandon*

Capital Crimes§

Dirty Work⋆

Blood Orchid‡

The Short Forever⋆

Orchid Blues‡

Cold Paradise⋆

L.A. Dead⋆

The Run§

Worst Fears Realized⋆

Orchid Beach‡

Swimming to Catalina⋆

Dead in the Water⋆

Dirt⋆

Choke

Imperfect Strangers

Heat

Dead Eyes

L.A. Times

Santa Fe Rules†

New York Dead⋆

Palindrome

Grass Roots§

White Cargo

Deep Lie§

Under the Lake

Run Before the Wind§

Chiefs§

COAUTHORED BOOKS

Jackpot⋆⋆ (with Bryon Quertermous)

Bombshell⋆⋆ (with Parnell Hall)

Skin Game⋆⋆ (with Parnell Hall)

The Money Shot⋆⋆ (with Parnell Hall)

Barely Legal†† (with Parnell Hall)

Smooth Operator⋆⋆ (with Parnell Hall)

T R A V E L

A Romantic's Guide to the Country Inns of Britain and Ireland (1979)

M E M O I R

Blue Water, Green Skipper

⋆*A Stone Barrington Novel*
†*An Ed Eagle Novel*
‡*A Holly Barker Novel*
§*A Will Lee Novel*
⋆⋆*A Teddy Fay Novel*
††*A Herbie Fisher Novel*

FOUL PLAY

STUART WOODS

G. P. PUTNAM'S SONS
NEW YORK

PUTNAM
— EST. 1838 —

G. P. PUTNAM'S SONS
Publishers Since 1838
An imprint of Penguin Random House LLC
penguinrandomhouse.com

Library of Congress Cataloging-in-Publication Data

Names: Woods, Stuart, author.
Title: Foul play / Stuart Woods.
Description: New York : G. P. Putnam's Sons, 2021. |
Series: A Stone Barrington novel.
Identifiers: LCCN 2021034294 (print) | LCCN 2021034295 (ebook) |
ISBN 9780593331699 (hardcover) | ISBN 9780593331798 (ebook)
Subjects: GSAFD: Suspense fiction. | Mystery fiction.
Classification: LCC PS3573.O642 F68 2021 (print) |
LCC PS3573.O642 (ebook) | DDC 813/.54—dc23
LC record available at https://lccn.loc.gov/2021034294
LC ebook record available at https://lccn.loc.gov/2021034295
p.   cm.

Printed in the United States of America
1st Printing

Book design by Kristin del Rosario
Title page art: Blurred rainy street © Drop of Light/Shutterstock

FOUL PLAY

ONE

Stone Barrington was headed down Second Avenue in the heaviest rain he could remember. Fortunately, he was in a taxi. He was also about a third of a block from his street. The traffic on the cross street had come to a complete halt, and thus, so had Second Avenue, and Stone had an appointment with a new client in five minutes.

"I think I'd better get out here," he said to the driver.

"What's that? I can't hear you." The rain was hammering on the cab's roof, making a horrific noise.

"I'm going to get out!" Stone shouted, shoving some money through the plexiglass screen.

"You're gonna drown!" the driver shouted.

"I have an umbrella!" Stone shouted back, opening the rear door. He stuck the umbrella out first and got it open, then he stepped into the street and kicked the door shut behind him. He was ankle deep in water, but he made it to the sidewalk, which was marginally better.

As he rounded the corner, the traffic on the cross street suddenly began to move, and turning onto his street, he looked up the block and saw a man kicking something on the sidewalk. His vision was not helped by the rain, but it looked as though a dog was being abused. Stone simultaneously started to trot and close his umbrella, wrapping the tab around it and securing it, while the rain began drumming on his hat. Then he realized that the lump on the sidewalk was a man.

"Hey!" Stone shouted at the kicker. The man looked up at him; he was wearing a ski mask. Stone ran at him—giving little thought to the size of the man, which was large—and drew back the umbrella. He swung at the man, connecting with his left arm, near the shoulder, and heard a shout of pain. The umbrella was golf-sized and had a thick wooden shaft, topped by a heavy, brierwood curved handle. Stone swung again, aiming at the head. The handle caught the man on the chin, but not solidly, since he was now withdrawing.

Stone thought of pursuing him, but the man on the ground let out a loud groan, gaining Stone's attention. He opened the umbrella and held it over the victim. "Can you hear me?" Stone shouted.

"Yes," the man said, nodding. Blood was being washed off his face by the rain.

"If I help you, can you get up?"

"Maybe."

Stone held out his left hand, and the man grabbed it and struggled to his feet. "Hold on to my arm," Stone said. "It's just a few doors." They shuffled up the street together, taking small steps. At the door, Stone found he couldn't ring the bell without letting go of the umbrella, so that was what he did. He leaned on the bell and heard a continuous ringing.

A moment later, Joan Robertson, his secretary, opened the door, sized up the situation, and took the man off Stone's hands. He grabbed the umbrella, closed it, and stepped inside.

"What happened?" Joan asked. "This man is bleeding."

"Just get him inside, make him as comfortable as you can, then call 911 and ask for an ambulance. Tell them a man has been beaten up, and ask for the cops, too."

B y the time help arrived, Joan had the man out of his raincoat and jacket, his tie was loosened, and he was sitting up in a chair in Stone's office, sipping from a mug of tea with an electric heater blowing on him. The EMTs arrived first and gave him a quick going-over.

"I don't think anything is broken," said the woman in charge of the team, "but it's a good thing you arrived when you did, or the man might have killed him."

The two cops stood by. "Our turn now?"

"Sure," the woman said. "He doesn't need to be transported.

Whatever the lady put in that tea is probably as good for him as anything we've got in the wagon."

Stone walked them to the door, while the cops started asking questions and taking notes. Soon they finished and took their leave.

All that Stone had heard of the conversation was the man's name. "You're Shepherd Troutman, is that right?"

"He's your eleven o'clock," Joan said. "He was on time, too." She had tucked a blanket around him.

"He looks like he's about the same size as Peter," Stone said, referring to his grown son, who lived in Los Angeles. "See if you can find him a robe in Peter's closet."

Joan headed upstairs to Peter's room, and Stone sat down on the sofa, across the coffee table. "Mr. Troutman, do you feel like talking a bit?" he asked.

"I guess I can rub a few words together and make simple sentences," he said. "But don't ask me to do any math."

"That's okay with me," Stone said, "but with all the excitement, I can't remember why we're meeting. Who sent you to see me?"

"My banker," Troutman said. "I'm new to the city, and I opened an account with him."

"Who sent you to the banker?"

"A guy who went to college with him, who was my last banker."

"What's the new guy's name?"

"Barton Crisp," he said.

"He's my banker, too, or one of them. You did well there."

"That was my instinct."

"Where'd you come to New York from?"

"Western Massachusetts."

"My family springs from that area," Stone said. "Hence my surname."

"Great Barrington? I'm from Lenox."

"Welcome to New York," Stone said. "We're normally more cordial than your reception this morning. Do you know who your assailant was, or why he attacked you?"

Troutman shook his head. "Right out of the blue. Never saw him before. Not that I saw him, with that mask on. I can't think of why anybody would attack me, except to rob me. I have a few hundred dollars in my pocket, but he didn't get that far before you came along. I haven't thanked you properly. I'm very grateful for your help."

"I'm glad I was there," Stone said. "Why the move to New York?"

"I've never lived anywhere but Lenox, but my father died a few months ago, and I sold the family business for a lot of money, so I thought I'd make a fresh start."

"Married?"

"Divorced, nearly two years ago."

"Might your former wife want to come at you again for more money?"

"No, she got a very favorable settlement at the time, and she's remarried."

"Where are you living in the city?"

"At the Carlyle Hotel, for the moment, but I want to find an apartment to buy."

Joan came back with a cashmere robe. "Mr. Troutman, if you'll change into this, I'll get your other things dried and pressed. There's a powder room where you can change right over there."

Troutman took the robe and excused himself.

Stone turned to Joan. "New client, new in town. Run off a copy of the list for him, will you?"

"Sure thing." She went back to her desk, printed out the document, and returned to Stone's office as Troutman did.

Stone took the document and handed it to his new client. "This is a list of names and addresses of people you might need to see or talk to at some point—doctor, dentist, insurance agent, financial adviser, real estate broker, etcetera."

Troutman looked through the list. "Thank you. I'm sure this will be very useful. I probably should see the financial adviser first, since I'm sitting on a lot of cash."

"If I may ask, how much did you derive from the sale of the business?"

"Two hundred sixty million, give or take," Troutman replied, "after taxes. And I got about that much from my father's estate. I was his only heir."

"In that case, I'll recommend a different financial adviser," Stone said, taking the list from him and writing in the name, address, and number of Charley Fox, his own adviser. "Charley is accustomed to dealing in larger sums than most brokers, and he's more creative in selecting investments. He handles all of my money."

"I'll call him today."

"There's another attorney on the list, Herbert Fisher, who works with me, and is usually available if I'm not. He works at our firm, Woodman & Weld, in the Seagram Building on Park Avenue at Fifty-Second Street. I work here, mostly."

They chatted for another half hour, then Joan brought Troutman his dried clothes, and he changed again.

"The rain has let up a lot," Stone said, handing him an umbrella, "but you'd better take this. Are you going to the Carlyle, now?"

"Yes."

"Joan, ask Fred to drive Mr. Troutman."

"That's very kind of you."

"We wouldn't want you to get all wet again, Mr. Troutman."

"Call me Shep," he said, shaking hands.

"Joan will put you in the car."

Joan came back a moment later. "Dino on one for you."

TWO

S tone picked up the phone. "Hey." Dino Bacchetti and Stone had been partners on the NYPD many years before. Now Dino was the police commissioner for the City of New York.

"My computer says that some of my uniforms just made a house call at your place. Tell me about it."

"I got out of a cab around the corner, made the turn, and saw a man—large, wearing some sort of raincoat and a ski mask and, come to think of it, a black baseball cap, kicking a man who was down. I hit him on the arm with my umbrella, then once on the chin, nearly missing, and he ran. The victim was my eleven o'clock appointment. Joan and I got him inside, and the rest is about as you would imagine."

"How badly was the victim injured?"

"He's ambulatory, but if I had gotten there a little later, he could have been dead. Are you keeping a watch on my place?"

"Not exactly. There's a note in the computer that says call me if a visit is made there or at my place."

"Thank you."

"Also, there was another such beating, about the same time—same description as the attacker at your place, but on the Upper West Side."

"Coincidence?"

"Maybe. I don't like coincidences."

"I seem to recall that."

"Well, it's too soon to panic. Dinner at P. J. Clarke's, seven?"

"Done." They both hung up.

Joan came in. "How'd it go with the new client?"

"Very nicely. I sent him to Charley Fox for advice."

"Oh, good. Sounds like he can pay our bill."

"He most certainly can."

"He said he's at the Carlyle. For how long?"

"He wants to look for an apartment."

"For a while, then. He's all alone in the big city?"

"Yes. Tell you what. Call him and ask him if he'd like to have dinner at P.J.'s at seven."

"Okay." Joan came back in a couple of minutes. "Yes," she said.

"Did you tell him where it is?"

"Yes, I remember that he's new in town."

"Of course you do."

"He says he'll wear dry clothes."

"That's good."

"I liked him," Joan said. "Seems like a good guy."

"So did I. That's why I asked him to dinner."

"He's going to need to meet women," Joan said.

"Let's not get ahead of ourselves," Stone said. "Anyway, when word gets around that he has as much money as he has, he'll be swamped."

"That much, huh?"

"That much."

S tone got to Clarke's a little early, and Dino arrived a little later. The bartender had already brought drinks for both of them.

"I invited somebody to have dinner with us," Stone said.

"What's her name?"

"Shepherd Troutman."

"That doesn't sound like a her."

"That's because it isn't. He's a new client."

"And you wanted to impress him that you know the police commissioner, is that it?"

"That's not it. How about we just tell him you're a cop."

"Okay. Why'd you invite him?"

"He's new in town and alone, and he got beat up this

morning outside my house. I thought he might enjoy dining with a view of something besides the inside of a hotel room."

"Okay, you're a prince," Dino said.

Stone looked toward the door. "Here he comes, I think."

He caught Troutman's eye and waved him over and introduced him to Dino. "Dino's a cop," Stone said. "He's the guy you call when you need some parking tickets fixed."

"I'll keep that in mind," Shep replied, shaking hands.

"You look a lot better than you're supposed to," Stone said. "How'd that happen?"

"Well, I was short on underwear, so I asked Fred to drop me at Bloomingdale's, where they have what I want."

"Okay," Stone said. "What does underwear have to do with your appearance?"

"After I got the boxer shorts, I started out of the store, and a woman at a makeup counter waved me over and said, 'You need help.' She held up a mirror, and I saw that she was right. So she spent about ten minutes doing stuff, and I looked human again, so I bought whatever she had used, so I can look human again tomorrow."

"Good idea," Dino said. "I heard about your incident this morning. On behalf of the NYPD, I apologize."

"Oh, I thought New York greeted everybody that way," Shep said.

"You seem pretty cheerful for somebody who got mugged recently."

"A couple of painkillers helped. They made me a little fuzzy around the edges for a few minutes, but I got over it. Oh, Stone, I may have found an apartment to buy."

"Good. Where?"

"The one I'm living in now."

"In the Carlyle?"

"The manager told me it was for sale."

"How much was he asking?"

Shep told him.

"I hope you didn't snap it up at that price," Stone said. "Look around a bit. Start with what else they've got for sale, and if you still like the one you're in, offer him less."

"How much less?"

"A third. He'll counter, then you'll finally agree. How big is it?"

"Two bedrooms, study, living room, kitchen, lots of closet space, beautifully furnished, including a grand piano."

"Do you play?"

"A little. The guy who owned it was a big-time Broadway producer. He died a couple of months ago."

"So the estate is selling it, not the hotel?"

"That's right."

"What's the monthly maintenance?"

"Maid service is included."

"No—real estate taxes, repairs, utilities, use of the gym, like that. Every apartment you would own has a monthly fee that covers those things. In hotels, it's particularly high, because of the services available."

"I guess I'd better ask about that."

"You might also offer to rent it for a few months, to give you time to get the lay of the land."

"Maybe." Shep looked across the room, where two nicely dressed women were being shown to a table. "Funny, I saw one of those ladies walking through the lobby when I left. She smiled at me."

"That's something else every high-end hotel has," Stone said. "Not that they'd ever admit it."

Shep's eyebrows went up. "No kidding? That good-looking?"

"Like your suite, they're very expensive, too," Stone said.

"After dinner, you two come by for a drink. See what you think of the place."

THREE

They finished their apple pie and coffee and went outside.

"Shep," Stone said, "you ride with Dino. Maybe he'll let you play with his siren."

They saddled up and drove to the Carlyle, at Seventy-Sixth and Madison Avenue. Shep led them into an elevator, slipped his key card into a slot, and the elevator closed and went up fast.

"I'm going to get a nosebleed," Dino said.

The car stopped, and they stepped into a handsome vestibule, facing double doors. Shep let them in.

"Wow," Dino said.

"That goes for me, too," Stone said. "You undersold the place." The rooms were large and the ceilings high. They walked across the living room, Shep pressed a button, sliding doors slid open, and they stepped onto a broad terrace, with handsome outdoor furniture scattered about. The view was spectacular—south over Manhattan, and all the lights were on. "Great place for cocktails before dinner," Stone said, "with the sun setting slowly into New Jersey."

They toured the other rooms, and they were beautiful. Stone particularly liked the study/library. "Lots of showbiz titles," he said, looking closer.

"Those come with the place," Shep said. "The manager said the only things the estate took out were some museum-quality paintings, which their decorator replaced with good but less expensive pieces." Shep led them back into the living room, pressed another button, and a mirror slid up, revealing a well-stocked bar. He poured them drinks.

Stone felt the heft of his whiskey glass. "Baccarat," he said.

"The estate is leaving the crystal, but they're keeping the silverware," Shep said. "Somebody in the owner's family wanted it."

"Do you know what maker and pattern?" Stone asked.

"I've got it written down somewhere," Shep said.

"Get on the Internet and do a search. You can be ready to serve dinner in a few days."

They took seats in the living room. "Shep, what are you going to do with yourself, now that you're a free man?" Stone asked.

"'Do'? You mean, like, work?"

"If you like."

"I'm enjoying doing nothing," Shep said. "Every morning, I have breakfast in bed, then I get up and walk over to Central Park and spend an hour there, just nosing around. I do some window-shopping on Madison, check out the galleries—I've already bought a couple of pictures; they're being framed—and in the evening I go to the theater or listen to whoever is entertaining downstairs."

"What did you do before your father died?"

"I was the chief operating officer of the family business. Dad was always chairman and president. I knew it well, when the buyer came calling."

"What sort of business was it?"

"We designed and manufactured machine parts, especially prototypes. Dad always said we were the best in the business, and I think he was right. We had seven plants around the world."

"Did you have any problems selling it?"

"Not a bit. I sold to one of our competitors. They had wanted it for years. Dad had talked a lot about what to do with it, how much to ask, how much to take, so I didn't have any problems."

"Sounds like you've led a gilded life," Dino said.

"Don't you believe it. I went to work on the shop floor the day after I graduated from Brown, and over the next thirty years I worked every job in the place. Didn't take much time off, either."

"Was your dad on your back all the time?" Dino asked.

"Not after he was sure that I'd be a good worker. Then he

would just turn me over to the next department manager, who'd put me to work. Dad and I had a drink every Friday evening to talk over my week. I usually had a few suggestions for him, and he took most of them."

Dino stood up. "Well, I have to get up and arrest people tomorrow, so I'd better get home. My wife, Viv, gets home from a business trip tomorrow, so I can't be hung over."

Stone got up, too. As they got to the front door, Dino said, "Shep, you'd better rest up because you're going to have one hell of a lot of sex, after the ladies see this apartment."

"That's good advice," Shep said.

"Avoid the ladies downstairs," Stone said. "If you can't stand it anymore, rent a room in the hotel, and tell them you're a traveling salesman. Don't ever bring one up here."

"I've never thought sex was something you should pay for," Shep said, "so I'll be okay."

Stone and Dino rode down together.

"It's going to be fun watching him," Dino said. "I hope he can handle it."

"He seems like a very capable guy to me," Stone replied.

FOUR

S tone was getting dressed the following morning when his cell phone rang. He picked it up. "Speak."

"It's Dino. Listen, last night when we were at Shep's apartment at the Carlyle, you remember that he said something about strolling in the park every morning?"

"Yeah. I was going to tell him not to stroll in the park at night, but I knew you'd be all over me for disparaging your department's work at keeping the citizenry safe, and a bunch of statistics about how much safer it is in the park than it used to be."

"All of that is perfectly true," Dino said.

"Maybe, except for the 'perfectly' part."

"Maybe you should have told him not to," Dino said.

"What's happened?"

"A park employee found him facedown in the grass, near the Bethesda Fountain. He's at Lenox Hill now, still unconscious. They found your card and mine in his pocket. I guess they liked mine better, because they called me."

"I'll get right over there," Stone said. He hung up and called down to Joan. "Get me a cab. I'll be down right away."

"Yes, sir!"

S tone presented himself at the ER desk a few minutes later. He gave the nurse his card. "You have a Shepherd Troutman here, with this card in his pocket. He's my client. May I see him?"

A resident came out of the ER, and the nurse flagged him down. There was a whispered exchange between them, then the nurse said, "This is Dr. Seitz. He'll take you up to Mr. Troutman's suite."

Stone followed the young man into the elevator, and they went to the top floor. The suite was one large room, with living room–type furniture at one end and Shep Troutman at the other, in a hospital bed, apparently asleep.

"These are pretty nice quarters," Stone said. "Do you treat all your ER patients so well?"

"No," the doctor said, "just the ones in custom-made suits with the police commissioner's card in their pockets."

"Right," Stone said. "May I wake him?"

"He came to about an hour ago, and he's been in and out since. Take a seat and wait for him to come around on his own. He might be having a nice dream."

"What are his injuries?"

"Just one: a lump the size of a hen's egg on the back of his skull. No fracture. The jury's still out on brain damage."

Shep's eyelids fluttered and he made an effort to sit up. The doctor found the remote control and sat him up a little.

"Stone?" Shep said. "What are you doing here?"

Stone sat down next to him. "You first. Have a look around and tell me what you're doing here."

Shep looked around. "Did the hotel put me in another room?"

"No, this is a several-thousand-dollars-a-day suite at Lenox Hill Hospital."

Shep made an effort to sit up further, then stopped. "Ow," he said, and his hand went to the back of his head. "That's quite a lump."

"You should have seen it when you checked in," the doctor said, "before we treated it."

"Dino called me half an hour ago," Stone said. "It seems you were found in Central Park this morning, unconscious, and his card was found in your pocket, along with mine. Not surprisingly the hospital called Dino, who called me. Do you remember how you ended up in the park this morning?"

The doctor gave Shep some water through a glass straw. "I

usually go to the park, but I don't remember doing that this morning."

"What's the last thing you remember?" Stone asked.

"I was in the park, but it was dark, so it must have been last night."

"That makes sense. I should have warned you against walking in the park late at night." Stone turned to the doctor. "May I see the contents of his pockets?"

The doctor pointed at the bedside table. "Top drawer," he said.

Stone opened the drawer and took out a plastic bag. It contained a wallet, a key card from the Carlyle, a Mercedes car key, and a gold money clip with his name engraved on it, empty.

"Were you carrying any cash?" he asked Shep.

"Yes, maybe a thousand dollars."

"How about a wristwatch?"

"Yes, a Rolex Submariner."

"He won't have any trouble pawning or selling that."

"It wasn't a standard Submariner," Shep said. "It was the fiftieth anniversary limited edition."

"How is that different from the standard Submariner?"

"It has a green bezel, and the numerals are a little larger."

A voice came from behind Stone. "I'll call it in."

Stone jumped and turned around to find Dino standing behind him. "Don't sneak up on me like that," he said.

"Oh," Shep said, "and it had my name engraved on the back. It was a gift from my father some years ago."

"That'll help," Dino said, then made a call on his cell phone.

Stone turned back to the doctor. "What's his prognosis?"

"Well, we'll want to hang on to him for a couple of days. If he doesn't die or have a grand mal seizure, then we can probably send him home."

"That's encouraging," Shep said.

"Yes," Stone said. "It's always encouraging when the patient doesn't die. I've had considerable experience with people who've been hit over the head. And none of them died, who didn't have a fractured skull, at least. The hospital may just want to sell you this room for a couple more days." He turned to the doctor. "You can have him one more night, then boot him out of here."

"I confirm Stone's diagnosis," Dino said.

"Are either of you a physician?" the doctor asked.

"Of course not," Dino said, with scorn. "We're just cops. But together, we've seen more skull damage than you've had hot meals."

"Possibly," the doctor said, making a note on Shep's chart.

Stone gave Shep another card. "Call me, and I'll have Fred here with the car to take you home."

A very attractive nurse came into the room with some medication.

Stone leaned over and whispered in Shep's ear. "At these prices, it's okay to hit on the nurses."

"Gotcha," Shep said. "Now, if you don't mind, I'm going to get some more sleep." He lay back and did just that.

D ino and Stone rode down on the elevator together. "Dino . . ."

"I know. You're going to ask me if there were any more muggings last night. Of course, there were, but none of them resembled this one, not the way the other two resembled each other."

"So, this doesn't count as another coincidence?"

"Of course not. Shep was practically acting on your instructions."

Stone knocked Dino's fedora off. "You dropped your hat," he said.

FIVE

tone went downstairs to his office the following morning, and Joan greeted him. "Fred is back," she said. "He picked up Mr. Troutman at the hospital and delivered him to the Carlyle at about ten o'clock."

"Good," Stone said. "The man needs some rest. Our city has not treated him kindly so far."

"Well," she said, "if he's living at the Carlyle, he ain't doing bad." The phone rang, and Joan picked up the one on Stone's coffee table. "The Barrington Practice. Hi, Dino." She pressed the hold button. "Dino on one."

Stone picked it up. "Good morning. Did you avoid a hangover this morning?"

"Yeah, a lot of good it did me. Now we've got a headache of

a different sort. Shep Troutman called me a few minutes ago to tell me there's a dead woman in his apartment."

"Oh, swell. Any details?"

"I'm in the car. We're just arriving at the hotel. Come on up here." Dino hung up.

"Call Fred and tell him to bring the car up," he said to Joan.

"What's wrong?" Joan asked.

"Shepherd Troutman has a dead woman in his apartment." He threw up his hands. "Don't ask because I don't know." He left his office and waited outside for Fred, who appeared in the Bentley shortly. Stone got in. "The Carlyle," he said.

"Right, sir. Everybody's going to or from the Carlyle this morning." They arrived.

Stone rode up in the elevator and walked into the vestibule to find a uniformed cop standing there, looking bored. "Morning, Stone." He jerked a thumb. "Everybody who is anybody is in there," he said.

"Thanks, Harry." Stone walked into the apartment to find Shep, dressed in pajamas and a robe, sitting on a living room sofa, next to Dino. There were two detectives sitting on the opposite sofa.

"Hi, Stone," Shep said, looking forlorn.

"Good morning, Shep."

"Not really."

"Okay, Shep," Dino said. "You can start now. Sorry for the delay."

"Just a minute, Dino." Stone turned to the detectives. "Sorry, fellas, you don't get to hear the first performance."

The detectives got up and trudged across the room toward the study.

"Okay, Shep. From the top."

"Okay," Shep said. "After I got back from the hospital, I went to bed. I was very tired, and I fell asleep quickly."

"What next?"

"I woke up maybe half an hour ago, maybe more, when I heard a woman screaming. At first, I thought she was out in the hall, but she was getting louder, and it was coming from the living room. I got out of bed and went in there to find the hotel maid, hysterical. I got her calmed down a bit, and she pointed down the hallway where the guest rooms are and said there was a dead woman in there. I went and checked, and she was right. In the first bedroom. You can see for yourself. She's still in there."

"In a minute," Stone said. "Did you touch her?"

"I walked over to her and put my fingers to her throat. She was cold to the touch, and I couldn't find a pulse."

"That's all? Did you disturb the room in any way?"

"No, I came back in here and asked the maid to make some coffee, just to calm her down, then I called Dino."

"You got anything to add to that, Dino?" Stone asked.

"Not yet. That's what he told me."

"Is everybody on the way?"

"The detectives are in the study. This place will be full of people in ten minutes."

"Then let's go look at Shep's guest before they get here."

"She's not my guest," Shep protested. "I never saw her before."

"I did," Dino said. "Let's go look.

Stone walked to the study door. "All right, fellas, you can come out, now. We're going to view the body, and you can watch, so you can see that we do it right."

They looked at Dino and Dino nodded.

Stone led the way into the bedroom. It was in good order, except that there was a green dress and some underwear and shoes on or around a corner chair, and there was a corpse in the bed. Naked, as it turned out, when Stone lifted the covers.

"You know her?" he asked Dino.

"I met her at the same time you did," Dino replied. "Two nights ago at P.J.'s. Well, we weren't exactly introduced. She and another woman walked past our table, and you, Stone, gave us a lecture on avoiding sin, as I recall."

"Ah, yes," Stone said. "I remember. Do you, Shep?"

"I guess it could be the same woman," Shep replied, walking over and looking at her more closely. "Yeah, it is. I didn't recognize her in the changed circumstances."

"That's understandable," Stone said. "Neither did I, at first."

A voice came from the door. "Okay, everybody, out of the way." The medical examiner, a large man carrying a black bag, bustled into the room and walked over to the bed. He pulled the covers back, looked over the body, listened to the chest with his stethoscope, then turned it over and examined it again, finally returning it to its original position. "This woman is dead," he said.

"Always the one for understatement, Leo," Dino said.

The ME produced a thermometer and inserted it into her anus, then read the numbers on an attached electronic accessory.

"Somewhere between six and eight hours." He took a small zippered bag from his larger one and did a vaginal examination, swabbing the area, then placing the swabs in a slim bottle and capping it. "She had sex before she died, maybe more than once, but there's no immediate appearance of semen. Preliminary cause of death, strangulation. I'll know more when I get her on my table, but that concludes my prelim. The investigator can have her now."

"Let's go back to the living room," Dino said, "and let the guys do their work."

"What work is that?" Shep asked.

"Looking for trace evidence, hairs and such," Dino said. "Don't you watch TV?"

"Can I put some clothes on?" Shep asked.

"Nope. The investigator is going to want a look at you, too. Let's go have some coffee."

They got their coffee and sipped it silently, until the crime scene analyst joined them. "Mr. Troutman," he said. "Have you showered or bathed this morning?"

"No," Shep replied.

"Please come with me, and we'll have a look at you." He led

Shep into his bedroom and closed the door. A few minutes later, the analyst returned. "Okay, your man's clean," he said. "He's showering now, and he wants you to wait for him."

Two attendants entered the suite with a gurney and departed with the body. The maid came back.

"Can I change the room, now?"

Dino nodded.

Stone poured them some more coffee, and eventually, Shep came out, dressed in a tracksuit. "Thanks for waiting," he said. "Where am I in all this?" he asked.

"Innocent," Stone said, "as far as I can tell."

"I agree," Dino said. "Your story is backed up by the maid, and the analyst didn't find anything. The murder occurred when you were still in the hospital."

"How did the woman and whoever killed her get in here?"

"My guess is she'd used this apartment before you moved in. She got ahold of a key card somehow, brought her trick up here, and delivered her service, then he strangled her and left."

"Why?"

Stone shrugged. "Maybe she asked for too much money, and that made him mad. These things should always be negotiated up front."

"Why was the maid here?"

"It's her job. She probably came in, called out for you and didn't get an answer, then went to work."

"Dino?" Shep asked.

"That's as good a guess as any. I mean, the guy didn't leave the cash on the dresser, and the analyst didn't mention finding any."

"Maybe I should go back to Massachusetts," Shep said.

"Don't deprive us of your company," Stone replied. "Statistically, I think you've used up all your opportunities to experience violence."

"I hope you're right."

"Were you thinking of going running?" Stone asked.

"Yes."

"Don't. You're recovering from a concussion, so you should just rest. Read a book or watch TV."

Dino rose. "I'll let you know if your Rolex turns up," he said.

"Take it easy the next day or two," Stone said, then they both left.

They got on the elevator. "I hope we don't hear from him again anytime soon," Dino said.

SIX

S tone worked through the day and at about quitting time, Joan buzzed. "Charley Fox on one," she said.

Stone punched the button. "Hey, Charley."

"Hey, Stone. I had a weirdo in here about an hour ago, said you sent him."

"The only person I've sent you recently is Shepherd Troutman."

"That's the guy. Is he nuts or what?"

"Why do you ask?"

"Well, he'd hardly sat down when he started telling me these stories—he was beaten up on the street, and again in Central Park. He found a dead hooker in his bed this morning, like that."

"Gee, Charley, why do you think that's weird? These things happen in the big city. How'd you leave it with him?"

"I told him to wire me some money to open an account, then we'd talk."

"Did he?"

"Did he what?"

"Wire you some money."

"I dunno. I haven't checked."

"Well, check it and call me back." Stone hung up.

A minute later, Charley called back. "I checked, and he wired me some money."

"How much?"

"Two hundred and fifty million dollars. A quarter of a billion. My bank confirmed it. What, is he crazy, wiring a stranger that kind of money?"

"I sent him to you, Charley. That's all you need to know about his character. Now do you think he's real?"

"I think his money is real."

"Well, everything else he told you was real, too. He's new in town, and he has the worst luck of anybody I've ever met."

"What am I supposed to do?"

"Figure out some investments for him, get his approval, and buy. That's what you do, isn't it? And while you're at it, get him to sign the documents making him a client. I wouldn't want you to get yourself arrested this early in the relationship."

"I'll call him right now." Charley hung up.

A few minutes later, Joan buzzed again. "Mike Freeman on

one." Mike Freeman was CEO of Strategic Services, the second-largest security company in the world, and a partner in an investment company, Triangle Investments, with Stone and Charley Fox.

"Hey, Mike."

"Hey, Stone. I hear Charley just picked up an interesting new client."

"Not interesting, fascinating."

"Did all that stuff really happen to him?"

"It did. I saw the results in all three cases."

"This gentleman sounds as if he needs some personal security services. Should I call him?"

"It's better if I call him, then get him to call you."

"I'll sit here, huddled by the phone."

"See you." Stone hung up. Almost immediately, Joan buzzed. "Shep Troutman on one."

"Hello, Shep."

"Hi, Stone. I went to see your friend, Charley Fox. I think he may have thought I was crazy. He hustled me out of there pretty quick, said he'd get back to me."

"That's my fault, Shep. I didn't brief Charley about you, so he wasn't quite ready."

"Well, I guess I might have thought I was crazy, too, if a guy like me walked into my office and told me about my recent experiences."

"Charley got your wire transfer, and he's already hard at work on an investment strategy for you. I suggest you make an appointment with him tomorrow and hear what he has to say. You'll need to sign some documents, too, to open your account with him."

"I had a message from him, but I haven't had a moment to get back to him."

"There's somebody else you might want to call, too, Shep."

"Who's that?"

"His name is Mike Freeman, and he's CEO of Strategic Services, a very large security company." Stone gave him the number.

"Do I need security?"

"I think the past few days have given us the answer to that question."

"You have a point," Shep said.

"I think you need a security plan, just as you need an investment plan: a couple of guys to spend some time with you for a while, figuring out what you need to do to stay safe."

"What sort of things?"

"How much cash do you carry around, Shep?"

"In New York? A thousand, fifteen hundred, I guess."

"You have credit cards?"

"An Amex and a Visa."

"Then you don't need anything in your pocket except enough for tips and cabs. You might also need a safety-deposit box and, when you find a place to live, a good safe installed."

"I found a place to live," Shep said.

"Great! Where?"

"Right where I am right now. I looked at some other apartments in the building, then I made them an offer. We haggled and settled on about a quarter less than they were asking."

"Congratulations, it's a beautiful place."

"Thank you."

"You'll want to beef up security on the place, though, after the most recent event."

"I'll call Mike Freeman."

"Something else: Do you own a car?"

"I drove my father's old Mercedes down here. I thought I might trade it in."

"Then get garage space thrown in with the apartment. Parking's expensive in New York."

"It's included in the deal."

"Good."

"Let's have lunch again in a few days and see if you need to do some more planning."

"There are a couple more things I need: a Joan and a Fred."

Stone laughed. "If you hired them away, I'd have to shoot you, or myself. Don't call an employment agency, though. I'll put them to work on finding you somebody."

"Fair enough. I'll talk to you later."

Stone hung up thinking Shep Troutman might yet survive living in New York City.

SEVEN

Stone was on a phone call when Joan came into his office and held up a note: SHEP. He excused himself from his present call and pressed the button. "Shep?"

"Good afternoon, Stone."

"Anything wrong?"

Shep laughed. "I guess you've become accustomed to talking to me only when terrible things have happened."

"Of course not. How can I help you?"

"I'm car shopping, and I was impressed with your Bentley. Are you pleased with it?"

"Very much so. If you decide you want one, I'll put you in touch with someone who can find it fast."

"I shouldn't just walk into a dealership?"

"You can certainly do that, but it's likely that they will have only one or two cars in stock. Then if you don't like the color or interior of one of those cars, you'll need to place an order and wait several months for delivery."

"How should I proceed?"

"First, go to the Bentley website and build yourself the perfect Bentley for you. Then send that description to a friend of mine, Herman Goldsmith, and ask him to find you something like that. He'll search the country and come up with existing new cars. If you like one of them he'll get it for you right away, and he'll usually give you a discount, which is something that's hard to come by with a dealer."

"I've had a talk with your people at Strategic Services, and they've suggested some armor. Yours is armored, isn't it?"

"Yes, and I bought it directly from them. They have a department that armors vehicles. Or Herman can find you a car, and you can give it to them for armoring."

"Would you say that armoring is worth doing?"

"Well, it's only saved my life twice—once in a horrific accident, the other from a man on a motorcycle with a gun."

"I guess I'll need to think about that," Shep said.

Stone gave him Herman's number, then hung up.

Near the end of the day, Joan buzzed. "Herman Goldsmith on one."

"Hello, Herman."

"Hi, Stone. I want to thank you for the customer, Shepherd Troutman."

"Sure. Did you find him something?"

"A gorgeous Flying Spur. He'll have it by noon tomorrow. Will his check be good?"

"You have nothing to worry about with Shep."

"He's trading in a Mercedes. My guy is looking it over now at the Carlyle."

"I haven't seen his car, but I know it belonged to his father. My guess is it doesn't have a lot of mileage on it."

"Good. Thank you again." Herman hung up.

Joan buzzed again. "Dino on two."

"Hey, Dino."

"Hey, yourself. Dinner at Patroon, seven o'clock?"

"Done. Is Viv here?" Viv was COO at Strategic Services, and she traveled the world a lot.

"Amazingly, yes. See ya." He hung up.

S tone slid into a booth with Dino and Viv. "You don't look jet-lagged," he said to her.

"I'm always jet-lagged," she replied. "You get used to it."

"How's our friend Shep doing?" Dino asked. "Any beatings or corpses in his life for the past couple of days?"

"It's as if none of that ever happened," Stone said. "He's buying his apartment at the Carlyle, and he bought a Bentley from Herman today. His disposition is sunny."

"Dino told me about Shep," Viv said. "Sounds like he should meet a friend of mine."

"Anybody I know?"

"No, she married into old money twelve years ago, and they lived mostly in the Hamptons. She's divorcing him."

"Sounds like something Herbie Fisher could do for her. Does she have a lawyer?"

"She's just at the point of taking that step. I'll tell her to call Herb."

"Is she a free woman, yet?"

"She has been for some time, but she was slow to get to the lawyer stage. I'm sure she'd be interested in meeting Shep, and she's already dug her gold, so no worries there for him. What's he like?"

"Good-looking, bright, articulate, well-dressed, in a conservative way. He's recently cashed out of a large family business."

"All admirable qualities in a man. Her name is Brooke Alley," Viv said, writing down her number and giving it to Stone, who pocketed it.

Dino accepted a fresh drink and a menu. "For the life of me I can't figure out how Shep Troutman got through life before he met Stone."

"Tell you what," Viv said. "Why don't I give a little dinner party soon, and I'll invite Brooke and Shepherd."

"Why not?" Stone asked. "You can seat them next to each other."

Viv pulled out her iPhone and went to her calendar. "How about, let's see, not tomorrow night, but the night after?"

"I'm free, and I'm almost sure Shep is." He got out his phone and called Shep.

"Hello, Stone."

"Hi, there, Shep. Are you free for dinner the day after tomorrow?"

"I certainly am. Where?"

"At Dino's house."

"Dress?"

"Hang on." He covered the phone "How are we dressing, Viv?"

"Black tie," she said. "Seven o'clock."

Stone told Shep, then gave him the address. "See you then."

"One thing, Stone: I've got a couple of security people tailing me. One of them will want to be in the apartment."

"Shouldn't be a problem. See you then." Stone hung up.

"And who are you bringing?" Viv asked.

"You mean, besides Shep?"

"He's not your date, he's Brooke's."

"Oh. I'll let you know tomorrow."

L ater, Stone had just crawled into bed when his cell phone rang. "Yes?"

"This is the White House operator, Mr. Barrington," a female voice said. "Will you accept a call from the president?"

"Certainly," he replied. A moment later, Holly Barker was on the line.

"Good evening," she purred. "I know you're well, so I won't ask. A friend of mine—lovely person—is coming to New York tomorrow. Can you put her up for the night?"

"I don't do less than two nights," Stone said. "Viv and Dino are having a dinner party at home the night after. Can your friend make that?"

"It will be arranged. My friend will see you tomorrow afternoon."

"It's black tie, and she will be very welcome," Stone said, but she had already hung up.

Stone called Viv's cell phone and was sent directly to voice mail.

"It's Stone. I have a date for your party. Expect a few Secret Service people to be hanging around, in addition to Shep's body man. See you then!" He hung up and was soon asleep.

EIGHT

S tone got to his desk at mid-morning and buzzed Joan.

"Yes, sir?"

"My friend from D.C. is coming in this afternoon."

"I'm aware."

"How the hell can you be aware? I just found out last night."

"I had a call earlier from the head of her Secret Service detail," she said.

"Oh."

"Where will you be dining?"

"Tonight, in the study. Tomorrow night at Dino's house."

"Got it," she said. "Anything else?"

"Call Shep and tell him we need his full name, date of birth, and social security number, then call Viv and tell her the same about Brooke Alley, then give the data to the Secret Service.

Also, ask Viv to get the same info on her security agent, who will be traveling with Shep, and add that."

"Got it."

They both hung up. Stone listened and could almost hear the hum of activity as everybody in the house began to get ready for the visitor.

A t five o'clock, Holly had not yet made an appearance, so he went upstairs to shower and change. He walked into the master suite and found the president of the United States sitting up in bed, naked, reading the *New York Times*.

"Good afternoon," she said brightly.

"It certainly is," he said, shedding clothing. In a moment, he was beside her, and everything unfolded exactly as it should.

A few minutes in, they took a breather and lay next to each other, panting a little.

"You didn't tell me there would be a murder suspect at dinner tomorrow night," she said. "The Secret Service is concerned."

"Then they should do a better job," Stone replied. "If they had, they would have known that he is not a suspect and that the murder occurred in his hotel suite while he was an inpatient at Lenox Hill Hospital. His personal information has already been conveyed to the Service, and the dinner party is being held at the home of the police commissioner of New York City, so they need have no concerns for your safety."

"It is their job to look askance at everyone attending such a social gathering," she said.

"And it is your job to pooh-pooh them now and then, when you know better than they, which you now do."

"Oh, all right."

"I would now like to exercise my constitutional right to petition the head of the United States government for another go at her."

"Your petition is heard and accepted, with pleasure," she said, holding out her arms.

The following morning, Holly disappeared into a black SUV, which drove her north to where she could begin her sacking of Madison Avenue shops, which awaited her arrival, by appointment.

Stone went to his desk and, almost immediately, Joan told him Dino was on line one.

"Good morning."

"Well, a not bad morning," Dino said. "My people found Shep Troutman's Rolex Submariner."

"Where?"

"Being worn by a player in a hot soccer match, in Central Park. When questioned he said he had bought it from somebody—he couldn't say who—on the street, for a hundred bucks."

"Great, you can present Shep with it at dinner tonight. I'd like to know more about who the guy bought it from."

"So would everybody else. All we got for a description was 'tall male.'"

"Well, I guess that eliminates short males. And all females."

"Your judgment is unerring."

"Is Viv working hard on tonight's soiree?"

"Well, yes. The character of the event has changed somewhat since she learned there would be a president at her table."

"It's not the first time. She can handle it."

"Yes, but instead of supervising our cook herself, she has engaged the fanciest caterer in the city to feed us. And she is dealing with a swarm of security people—hers, mine, Shep's, and enough Secret Service agents to fill a medium-sized school bus. She's also trying to figure out how to hide them where nobody will notice them during drinks and dinner."

"Good luck with that. Just stuff them all into the kitchen."

"Then the caterer will walk out in a huff," Dino said, "and Viv will divorce me."

"You should have bought a larger apartment."

"Don't mention that to Viv. My last interior decoration experience was so painful I have resolved never to move again."

"Surely she will freshen things up now and then."

"Yeah, but if she wants, say, new curtains, she'll have to smuggle the decorator in when I'm at work, and when they're ready to hang the curtains, too. Then I'll catch hell for not noticing them for a month."

"It's an unwinnable war," Stone said. "Maybe it's better to just surrender."

"What the hell do you think I'm doing? I keep a white flag in my pocket."

"I gotta go."

"Bye."

They both hung up.

Holly made her entrance around five, followed by an over-loaded Secret Service agent and Fred, staggering under the bulk of boxes and shopping bags.

Holly accepted a martini in the study. "I solved my dilemma about what to wear tonight by buying five dresses," she said, taking a gulp. "But now I have to decide which one to wear."

"I'm wearing black," Stone said. "Start from there."

"Clever you." She tucked an olive into her cheek, then kissed him.

"Tastiest kiss ever," Stone said. "I believe there's an anchovy in that olive."

"At the very least." She swallowed the olive and kissed him again.

"Can I get you another olive?" he asked.

"Please."

NINE

Stone and Holly were the first to arrive, since Holly wanted to avoid making an entrance. They were quickly supplied with alcoholic beverages and had already begun to consume them when Shepherd Troutman was escorted into the living room by the rent-a-butler. He took Holly's offered hand. "You look exactly like what's-her-name," he said, hanging on to the hand.

Viv helped. "That's because she *is* what's-her-name," she said, freeing the hand.

"Call me Holly," she said. Then to Viv: "Get this man a drink, before he faints."

"I was just thinking of doing that," Shep said to Holly.

"Fainting?"

"Drinking. There seems to be a lot of it going on around

here." He turned to Viv. "I don't think we've met, so I'm just going to take a wild leap: you're Mrs. Bacchetti."

"Not at my own dinner parties. Viv will do nicely."

"And I'm Shep."

"I guessed."

There was a stir around the front door. "Here comes your date," Viv said to Shep. "Try and look impressed."

"That's easy," Shep said, eyeing Brooke Alley, clearly thinking she was a knockout in that strapless dress. His eye was drawn to where it was supposed to be.

"That's impressed enough," Viv whispered, then introduced them.

Brooke was even more astonished to meet Holly than Shep had been.

Viv did a little sheepherding, and Shep and Brooke found themselves by a window, talking to each other.

"What do you do, Shep?" Brooke asked.

"Absolutely nothing," Shep replied.

"I like a man who knows how to do nothing stylishly."

"Style is all I've got."

"I don't believe that for a moment," Brooke said, looking him up and down, while he stole another glance at her décolletage.

"You make that dress look wonderful," Shep said.

"See what I mean? Viv, is this what it's like in the free world?"

"No, just at my house. I've groomed him carefully. Excuse me for a moment, there's a clot of security people over there, and I have to go redistribute them." She shooed them into the kitchen, then grabbed the detail chief of the Secret Service. "I want you to herd these people into the breakfast room over there, where there is seating for eight, and only let them make rounds one at a time, and around the edges of the room. Is that clear?"

"Yes, ma'am," the man said, deferentially.

Viv thought he was clearly angling for a job at Strategic Services when he retired.

"Give me a call when you're a couple of weeks from retirement," she said, checking his name on the list.

D ino sidled up to Stone. "Talk to me. Nobody else will."

"Look at Shep," Stone said, watching him move back to Holly's side. "He doesn't have to be so fucking charming."

"Presidents bring that out in some men."

"And that friend of Viv's is a knockout. Why didn't she introduce her to *me*?"

"You're not the odd man tonight, nor the new guy in town," Dino explained. "Viv knows what she's doing. See how she's emptied the room of security people, except for one, over there behind the potted plant?"

When they were called to dinner, Stone was annoyed to find that Shep's place card, not his own, was between his putative date's and the president's.

As the first course was beginning to be served, Stone looked across the table at Dino, whose left index finger had gone to his ear, indicating a listening device there.

Dino looked at Stone, made a motion toward the front door with his head, and left the table.

Stone followed Dino to the elevator, where he was holding the door open.

"Are you armed?" Dino asked Stone.

"No."

Dino lifted a leg and unholstered a small semiautomatic. "It's only a .380," Dino said, "so if you have to use it, go for the head shot."

"What the hell is going on?" Stone asked.

"Some sort of problem with your guy Fred," Dino said. "He seems to want to shoot people."

"Then they must need shooting," Stone replied.

The elevator disgorged them into the lobby, where a doorman discretely pointed out the front door.

Stone followed Dino out onto the sidewalk, where Fred was wedged between two much larger men, holding his arms.

"You'd better call those guys off, before Fred hurts them," Stone said.

"Stand down," Dino said, and the two men freed Fred and stepped back.

One of them held up a Glock. "We got this off him," the man said.

"Give it back to him," Dino said quietly. "Tell us about it, Fred."

"I'm sorry, Commissioner," Fred said, tucking away his firearm. "The building was approached by two men from the direction of Park Avenue, where they had got out of a black car. Both were carrying, and I judged them to be up to no good."

"Where are these two men now?" Dino asked his men.

They looked embarrassed. "When they saw the Glock they got back into their car," he said, "and left in a hurry."

"That was my intended use of the pistol," Fred said. "I didn't expect to have to shoot anybody, but I was ready to do so if necessary."

"Good job, Fred," Dino said. He looked around. "Anything further?" he asked. No one spoke. Dino nudged Stone toward the front door. "Our dinner is getting cold," he said.

Once back in the elevator, Dino held out a hand. "My piece," he said.

Stone gave him back the .380.

"If Fred ever leaves your employ," Dino said, tucking the pistol back where it belonged, "I'd like to hear about it."

"You're not first in line," Stone said.

"Yeah? Who else?"

"Viv asked a long time ago."

"I've got to watch that woman every minute."

"Don't even try," Stone said. "She's too far ahead of you."

TEN

Stone settled in next to Brooke Alley, who was talking to Shep on her other side, and long enough for him to fully appreciate what was on display. She turned back without catching him at it. "Well, now," she said, "Viv tells me you are Stone Barrington, an attorney."

"I cannot deny any of that."

"Are you a free man?"

"I am when our president is not in town."

"How often does she come?"

"You don't really expect me to answer that, do you?"

Brooke smiled. "Sorry. How often does she visit New York?"

"Periodically, but not predictably."

"Just to see you?"

"I can't flatter myself to that extent."

"What do you do when she's not in town?"

"The best I can."

"And I'll bet that's pretty good."

"It's flattering that you should think so."

"I think you and I might do very well together."

"Well, since Viv threw this bash for the express reason of getting you together with Shep, we might run afoul of her good nature if we pay too much attention to each other. And she carries a gun at all times, you know."

"I didn't know."

"It's her business that requires it, not necessarily her nature."

"I'm relieved to hear it."

"Did I hear you mention the 'free world' earlier."

"One free of a husband," she said. "By the way, thank you for the recommendation of Herb Fisher as an attorney. We've already had a meeting."

"Not losing any time."

"Once unhitched, I move at a gallop."

"Your former stablemate isn't jealous?"

"More like relieved. He practically set the barn afire to get me moving. A quick stroke of the crop across the rump sped me up."

"For future reference, is that a preference?"

"That sounds like an Ogden Nash verse."

"And that sounds like an evasive answer, but I won't press."

"A press in the right spot is always welcome."

"I'll need guidance," he replied.

"I doubt that."

"Is it getting warm in here, or is it just me?" Stone asked, dabbing at his forehead with his napkin.

"It's not just you," she said, dabbing at her bosom.

"So nice to be in sync," he said.

"Tell me," she said, "what is your favorite characteristic in a lover?"

"Enthusiasm," he said without hesitation.

"Well, you're halfway there."

"I look forward to the other half."

"Do you think there's a vacant bedroom around here?" she asked.

"Probably, but the place is lousy with security, so I doubt if we could get away with it."

"Why so much security, I wonder? Does it mean that something terrible is about to happen?"

"No, it's just that everybody here—but you and I—has at least two of them in tow. The lobby downstairs looks like a police convention without the cigar smoke." He felt a tug at his coat pocket.

"That is my number," she said, "for a future occasion."

"Good, but only after Viv has cleared us to land."

"I'll take care of that," Brooke said.

Stone dropped his own card into her lap, and she swiftly transferred it from under her napkin to her bosom.

"And there is the fact that your date is my client," Stone pointed out.

"I'm not picking up a lot of heat from that direction. My guess is that any attempt at a pass will be perfunctory and easily blocked."

"In that case, I think an interception would be in order. But again, the coach must call the play."

As if by some secret signal, the two ladies rose and vanished into another room somewhere.

Shep turned to him. "Brooke is nice, don't you think?"

"Very much so."

"Not really my type, though. You should look into that."

"That's gracious of you, Shep."

"She's too good to go to waste."

"I agree."

"Well," Shep said, "I'm glad we got that out of the way."

The ladies returned from their visit, and Viv sat down next to Stone. "I think I was wrong about Shep and Brooke," she said. "When Holly hits the road, you should call her."

Stone nodded sagely but said nothing.

ELEVEN

S tone was at his desk the following morning when Fred came into the office. "The president has departed," Fred announced.

"I know. We said our goodbyes a bit earlier."

"You wanted to see me, Mr. Barrington?"

"Yes," Stone replied. "Please have a seat."

Fred looked a bit alarmed. "Something I've said or done?" he asked. "Last night, perhaps?"

"No, Fred, nothing like that. You always conduct yourself correctly."

"I'm relieved you think so, sir," he said, sounding relieved.

"I do. About last night: What did you make of the two armed men who got out of the black car?"

Fred gazed off into the middle distance, as if a photograph

of the men were being projected onto an unseen screen. "Six-three, two forty, mostly muscle. Not twins, but perhaps brothers; accustomed to dispensing violence, but not receiving it. I believe that one of them—take your pick—was the man you dispatched with your umbrella during that thunderstorm that gave us Mr. Troutman."

"Unaccustomed to receiving violence, you said?"

Fred nodded. "One more accustomed to being struck would have relieved you of that umbrella and stuck it up your arse—you should kindly excuse the expression."

"I'll keep that in mind, should we meet again."

"Oh, I believe you will meet again, sir. Last night's instance convinced me of that. They were delivered to that place by the black Mercedes S550, which waited to collect them when their task was done."

"And their task?"

"To deal with you, sir."

"Not Mr. Troutman?"

"Oh, no, sir," Fred said quickly. "They didn't appear from the direction from which he came. It appeared as though they had followed the Bentley. When they emerged, they took a close look at it, presumably to verify it was your car. No, I'm convinced you were the target. Mr. Troutman was likely a distraction, stumbled upon while he awaited your arrival. Had they made their point last evening, you would have been fortunate that neither of them was carrying an umbrella."

"Ah, um . . . and you think they'll try again."

"Oh, yes, sir. Between the two of us we've ruined their evening twice. I think they'll have been quite annoyed at that. I would suggest that you go armed at all times for a while, and that I accompany you for, ah, accuracy."

Fred was a two-time Royal Marine pistol champion, Stone reflected, and he, himself, was not. "Suggestion accepted," he said.

"And no strolls, sir. We'll take the Bentley. I mean to say, sir, the Bentley is armored, and you are not."

"Point taken."

"May I persuade you to wear that very nice armor vest that you never wear when you should? I know it ruins the line of your jackets, but nevertheless—"

"I'll think about it," Stone said, cutting him off. "Any thoughts on why they chose me for a beating? Twice?"

"Well, the first time you were carefully chosen—perhaps their employer bears some sort of grudge. Anyone like that in your recent past, sir?"

"I'll think about that, too. And last night?"

"Because they failed the first time."

"And why the simultaneous, apparently random attack on the West Side?"

"I think 'apparently' is the key word there. A distraction, I expect."

"All right, Fred, I'll mull over all that, and you and I will travel in tandem for a while. Good morning."

Fred nodded and left.

Stone picked up his phone and called Dino.

"Bacchetti."

"I've just had a chat with Fred," Stone said. "He has a number of opinions about last night." He enumerated them.

"Sounds about right to me," Dino said. "Somebody is always pissed off at you. It's something in your manner."

"Are you saying that I come off as superior?"

"No, more as a superior asshole," Dino said. "Not always, though. You're quite charming with women. I watched your performance with Brooke last night, and I admired it."

"I was mostly on the receiving end of that one," Stone admitted.

"Have you called her, yet?"

"No, the chopper has not even cleared the pad, yet. I'll have to restrain myself a little longer."

Joan buzzed. "A Ms. Alley, on two."

"Got it," Stone said. "Dino, I'll call you back." He hung up and pushed line two. "Good morning."

"Good morning," she said. "As the bootleggers used to say, 'Is the coast clear?'"

"Barely," Stone replied.

"Can I buy you dinner tonight?"

"No, but I'll buy you dinner."

"Shall we meet at Caravaggio, at seven-thirty?"

"We shall."

"I'll wear another low-cut dress," she said. "You seemed to so appreciate the one last evening."

"I'm a connoisseur of décolletage," he replied, "and I'll look forward to a new experience."

"Until seven-thirty, then."

"Confirmed." He hung up and called Dino.

"Bacchetti."

"Sorry about that."

"It was Brooke, right?"

"It was."

"I guess she couldn't restrain herself any longer."

"Either that, or she has a spy at the East Side heliport."

"I wouldn't put it past her."

"Neither would I."

"Now, to this other business of last night—the one with the armed muscle. Do you agree with Fred's analysis of the situation?"

"I'm not sure, but I don't have a better idea, so I'll take his recommendations for the time being."

"Where are you dining?"

"Caravaggio. Her choice."

"Oh, good, there'll be a mobster or two there, and that tends to quell small arms fire. Shooters don't like being shot back at."

"I hadn't thought of it that way, but I think you might be right."

"*Might* be right?"

"Don't push your luck."

"Would you like Viv and me across the room for backup?"

"Fred will be on the job. Besides, Viv will know what happens before I do."

"She's like that," Dino said.

TWELVE

Stone was just ordering a sandwich for lunch at his desk when Dino walked in. Stone pressed the intercom. "We have a guest for lunch," he said.

Joan came into the room with a pad and pencil. "What would you like, Commissioner?"

"What's he having?"

"A Reuben and a beer."

"Double up on that order," Dino said, and Joan left.

"Have a seat. What brings you to the upper atmosphere of the East Side?"

"Oh, I haven't choked on the carbon dioxide for a while. It always brings back memories."

"Of what?"

"Of choking."

"Of course."

"Our conversation of this morning led me to treat the events of last night as more of a police matter."

"How so?"

"Well, I reasoned that in such a tony neighborhood—mine—with such distinguished inhabitants—me—there might be a security camera or two at the corner of Sixty-Third and Park."

"And were there?"

"There were seventeen."

"Oh, good, so you'll have everything, including their dental X-rays."

"Not quite. We got a lot of shots of the car, which was, as Fred noted, a Mercedes S550 four-door sedan. With darkened windows, however, so we don't know who was inside."

"But you got shots of the license plates, right?"

"Sort of."

"Were any of the cameras high-definition?"

"All of them."

"Then why 'sort of'?"

"We got a usable partial plate, that's all."

"How usable?"

"The first four characters were '1PCT.' That's all we got."

"And how many vehicles in New York City begin with those characters?"

"New York State: a little under two thousand. Due to technical difficulties, we could not narrow the search to the city."

"What kind of 'technical difficulties'?

"Technical difficulties that were explained to me, but I didn't understand."

"Ah, that kind."

"Right."

"So we can't just go to the owner's residence and hammer on the door."

"We cannot."

"Well, did the attentions of the NYPD produce anything remotely useful?"

"We were able to use the feds' facial recognition software on the two thugs," Dino said.

"And?"

"And it didn't recognize them."

"Technical difficulties?"

"How did you know?"

"Just a wild guess."

"Don't get sarcastic."

"That wasn't sarcasm, it was irony."

"If you say so."

"I do."

Their lunch arrived in time to save Dino any further embarrassment.

———————

Dino polished off his beer, belched, and sat back in his chair. "I guess we're going to have to resort to old-fashioned police work," he said.

"What sort of 'old-fashioned police work'?"

"I'm going to have two cars following you at all times."

"Well, that should be easy, since I'm right here in this office most of the time."

"This will be rolling surveillance," Dino said.

"Okay, as long as it isn't black SUVs with blue flashers mounted on the dashboard."

"You got something against our police vehicles?"

"Yes. They look like police vehicles."

"What do you suggest?"

"I suggest unmarked sedans."

"I wonder if we still have any of those."

"What do detectives ride in these days?"

"Unmarked sedans, but this is not proper work for detectives. Patrolmen can handle it."

"Uniformed patrolmen?"

"Sure. You object to that, too?"

"Same objection as for the SUVs."

"You're getting ironic again."

"Dino, these patrolmen go to mass on Sunday or synagogue on Saturday, right?"

"Sure, most of them."

"What do they wear on those occasions?"

"Suits, I guess."

"There you go. No shopping or expense involved, just have them wear their own suits. They can pretend they're detectives. They'll like that."

"I guess you want me to issue them gold badges, too?"

"They can just pin the tin ones to their underwear."

"Anything else?"

"Yes: no heavy black shoes with white socks. That's always a tip-off."

"You'll get whatever they wear to mass or synagogue."

"I'll settle for that."

"What time is your dinner date?"

"Seven-thirty."

"My guys will be outside at seven."

"Fine, but not right in front of the house. Tell them to employ subtlety at all times."

"Why wouldn't they?"

"Because they're street cops. Don't you remember what that was like?"

"Dimly."

"I don't think we'll need to bust anybody tonight. All we need is a good license plate to work with."

"Suppose these people commit a crime?"

"Like what?"

"Like shooting you."

"Then they can bust them, right after they call the EMTs."

"I'll make a note of that," Dino said, making a note of it. "Is lunch over?"

"It is, unless you'd like a slice of blueberry pie, à la mode."

"I would like that."

The pie came, Dino ate it, then left without another word.

Stone pressed the intercom: "Joan?"

"Make sure that Dino doesn't wander into the street and get run over by a car."

"Yes, sir."

THIRTEEN

At seven-fifteen, Stone walked out the front door of his house and found Fred in the Bentley, with a black four-door sedan parked tightly at each end.

"Fred."

"Yes, sir?"

"I'm afraid Dino has gone a little nuts. He has two cars assigned to us, and I asked that they keep their distance, but you see."

"I see, sir. I'll have a word with them when we get to the restaurant."

"Fine."

"Sir?"

"Yes?"

"What restaurant are we going to?"

"Caravaggio, in the seventies. We've been there."

"Right, sir." Fred backed up until the Bentley's rear bumper made contact with the car behind, the driver of which immediately started it, reversed, and left enough distance for Fred to back up and pull out. "Do they know where we're going, sir?" Fred asked.

"They should, if Dino has told them. If they don't, they can just follow you."

"Yes, sir." They drove away.

"Pay no attention to the cops. Keeping up is their problem."

"Yes, sir."

Fred pulled up to the restaurant at the stroke of seven-thirty. Stone got out and left Fred to explain to the cops about not crowding him and not looking like cops. As he went inside, it occurred to Stone that he had not mentioned the cops' haircuts to Dino.

He gave the coat-check lady his coat and looked around for Brooke Alley. He sat down at the bar to wait and ordered a Knob Creek on the rocks. After a few minutes the headwaiter approached.

"Good evening, Mr. Barrington."

"Good evening, Gianni."

"Are you meeting someone?"

"Yes. Her name is Brooke Alley."

"Ah."

"'Ah'?"

"She tends to run late."

"I noticed. How late?"

"About half an hour," he replied.

Stone ordered another drink. At the stroke of eight, Brooke appeared, not looking flustered.

Stone helped her off with her coat and gave it to the coat-check girl. "Did one of us get the time wrong?" he asked Brooke.

"Is that a sly way of asking why I'm late?"

"Not sly enough, apparently."

"A woman needs a little leeway," she said, and they were led to a good table and seated with a view of the whole restaurant.

Brooke asked for a martini. Stone ordered it and nothing else.

"Aren't you drinking?" she asked.

"I've already had two."

"Oh, all right, I'm sorry I'm late."

"Thank you."

"I had hoped the décolletage might soothe your impatience."

"The décolletage is not soothing, but stimulating."

"I'm not sure how I could have improved on it."

"Nudity, perhaps."

"That's good. You're more yourself, now."

"A couple of drinks will do that for me."

Brooke laughed. "I thought the dress would get me off the hook."

"If there is a hook involved, I will deal with it later."

She laughed again.

He liked it when she laughed; her breasts moved.

"Okay, time to gaze into my eyes," she said.

"They're lovely eyes," he said, adjusting his field of vision upward.

"What color are they?"

"Gray," he ventured.

"Some would say hazel."

"I won't quibble."

Her martini came, and she took a gulp. "Gotta catch up," she explained.

"No rush." A menu was brought; everything was high Italian.

"I'll have the seafood risotto," she said.

Stone held up two fingers to the waiter.

"Can't you speak?" she asked.

"Just barely. And a bottle of the Bâtard-Montrachet," he said to the sommelier.

"Do you look at the prices, or just the names?" Brooke asked.

"Just the names."

"Because that wine has a breathtaking price next to it."

"It's a breathtaking wine," he replied.

They had finished their dessert and were on espresso.

"Would you like a nightcap at my place?" Brooke asked.

"I would like nothing better."

They got their coats on and left the restaurant. Fred was braced next to the rear door of the Bentley, and the two police cars were parked discretely on the opposite side of the street.

"Oh," Brooke said, tugging at his sleeve. "We won't need the car. I live right there." She pointed at the first awning.

"Fred, I think you can send our escort home. Come to think of it, you can go home, too."

"Oh, I couldn't do that, sir," Fred replied. "The commissioner would have me arrested. My instructions are to stick with you, no matter where you go."

"I've got a better idea," Stone said. "Stick with the car. I'll be a while."

He followed Brooke to her building, which turned out to be not apartments, but a townhouse, beautifully furnished.

"Your home is beautifully furnished," Stone said.

She hung up their coats in a hall closet. "My job in my marriage was to choose houses and decorate them," she said. "My husband's job was to pay for them. Making money was the only thing that interested him, and he didn't care what I spent."

He had thought they would sit in the living room, but she continued toward the rear of the house and into a large master suite.

"Now you can deal with the hook," she said, turning her back to him.

Stone dealt with it quickly, and the dress fell into a puddle around her feet. As it turned out, the dress had been the only thing she was wearing.

FOURTEEN

A ray of sunshine settled on Stone's brow, causing him to blink and look around. He was in a half-empty bed, his suit was folded neatly on a nearby chair, and there were shower noises coming from somewhere. He sought out the bathroom and let himself into the shower with her.

"Plenty of room for anything," she said over her shoulder. He tested her theory, which turned out to be correct.

She toweled him off, something he enjoyed, and dried his hair. "Would you like a shave?" she asked.

"Perhaps another time," he replied. "I've just got time to get home before breakfast arrives in my bedroom."

"And who delivers it?"

"A dumbwaiter. Would you like to join me for breakfast?"

"It would take me too long to dress," she said.

"After last night, I should think you could dress in seconds."

"But there's hair and makeup," she said. "All those things."

He dressed and got out of there. Fred, bless his heart, was snoozing away in the driver's seat, and the cops were nowhere to be seen. Fred awoke as he opened the rear door. "Sorry to keep you waiting so long," Stone said.

"Quite all right, sir," Fred replied, starting the car. "I slept quite well."

"That's an awful lie, Fred. When we get home, you go straight to bed. Orders."

"Yes, sir."

S tone arrived in his bed less than a minute before breakfast came. He switched on the TV, to the local news channel. He got the tail end of a report of a beating at Seventy-Sixth and Park Avenue, a block from the Carlyle. He called Dino.

"Bacchetti."

"I saw a report of a beating on Park at Seventy-Sixth. Please tell me it wasn't Shep Troutman."

"Funny you should mention that," Dino said.

"Oh, no."

"No, it wasn't Shep, but there's a theory that whoever beat the guy up thought he was. The same description would work for both, and the location said 'Shep,' too."

"Any witnesses?"

"None. The cameras are being checked as we speak, and detectives are talking to the victim at Lenox Hill."

"Keep me posted, will you? This is too creepy to be a coincidence."

"Why did you dismiss my guys last night, after all the trouble I went to?"

"Turns out, my date lives next door to the restaurant. I thought they'd be pleased."

"Actually, they were pleased."

"By the way, if you want them to pass for ordinary citizens on the East Side, you need to find them a new barber."

"That skin-on-the-sides look doesn't work uptown, huh?"

"Let's put it this way: if you'd had that haircut when you applied to buy your apartment, your co-op board would never have let you in the front door."

"I suppose you're right. It's going to take a few weeks to grow."

"I'll leave the growth rate in your capable hands. Now, can I finish my breakfast?"

Dino hung up, and Stone finished his breakfast.

A half hour later, as Stone was finishing the *Times* crossword, his phone rang. "Hello?"

"It's Shep. It wasn't me this time."

"I already checked with Dino. He'd had the same thought. The victim even looked a little like you."

"It's creepy."

"My thoughts exactly. Would you like to revisit your thoughts about who might have it in for you?"

"I have already done so. I came up with zilch."

"My other line is ringing. It must be Dino."

"Bye."

Stone picked up. "What do you hear?"

"The same Mercedes, or an identical one, was parked across the avenue, and the license plate was masked."

"They've heard of cameras, huh?"

"I guess criminals are getting smarter. Maybe Fred was wrong, and they were never after you. I think Shep must have made an enemy or two."

"I just talked to him; he swears not. Anyway, he's such a pleasant guy. He doesn't seem to be the type to make enemies."

"Enemies aren't picky," Dino said. "They choose their victims from a wide range. It's more to do with their own personalities."

"You're practically a shrink, you know that, Dino?"

"I get more traffic than your average headshrinker."

"I guess you do, at that."

"Dinner at P.J.'s tonight? Viv is off again this morning."

"Sure."

"Maybe I'll have more on the case by then."

"I hope so."

They both hung up.

FIFTEEN

Stone and Dino were in the midst of demolishing their steaks, when Shepherd Troutman appeared at their table.

"May I join you for a few minutes?" he asked.

"Of course."

A waiter produced another chair.

"Would you like to order something, Shep?"

"No, I had something earlier. First, I want to apologize to you both."

"Apologize? For what?"

"I wasn't entirely frank with you about my recent past. I thought I could handle it on my own, but I can't."

"Start at the beginning," Stone said.

"A couple of weeks after my father's death, a lawyer appeared at my office who said he had a client who was interested in buying the business. I thanked him and asked him to submit his client's offer to my attorneys, and I would get back to him. He said that his client didn't work that way, and he pulled a sheet of paper from his briefcase which had a number printed on it. It was for $250,000,000.

"I said it was an interesting offer, but that I would need the details in a written document. He produced a suitcase, like a military footlocker, set it on my conference table and opened it. It was full of cash, and he said it contained twenty-five million dollars, which would serve as a deposit. I had never seen that much money before."

"Neither has anybody else," Stone said, "except maybe somebody at the Federal Reserve."

"He said the rest would be wire transferred to a bank of my choice as soon as I had signed a document, which he produced. It was short and sweet, too much so. He wanted to leave the twenty-five million dollars in my safe, once I had signed the document."

"Let me stop you right there," Stone said. "There is a one hundred percent probability that anyone who has possession of that much money in a footlocker did not earn it by the sweat of his brow, nor did he obtain it by other means that are honest and aboveboard."

"That thought occurred to me, and once again, I told him to produce a written offer that my attorneys could review and I would, after they did, have them get back to him. He continued to insist that I keep the money in the footlocker, until I said that I could have the police inspect it and determine its origins, and that I would not sign the document he offered me." He took a sheet of paper from his pocket. "Here is a copy of the document."

Stone read it, which didn't take long. "I'm so glad you didn't sign this or accept the money. It sounds as though his 'buyer' was trying to implicate you in a criminal transaction that would allow him to blackmail you into selling your company cheaply."

"I expect so," Shep replied. "Finally, the man took his footlocker and left. I observed him through my office window, putting it into a van and driving away."

Dino spoke up, "Did you, by any chance, make a note of the license plate number of the van?"

"No, it was too far away to be legible."

"Did you hear from him again?"

"Yes. The following day he appeared at my office with a cashier's check on a Swiss bank for twenty-five million dollars, and a thick document detailing his client's offer."

"Did you keep the check?"

"No, I made a copy of the check and returned the original to him. I told him that I would send the contract to my attorney and respond to it after a few days. I also gave him my attorney's card and told him that any further communications with his buyer should take place between him and my attorney, that I would have nothing further to do with any transaction until my attorney was satisfied that it was, as you put it, 'kosher.'" He handed over the copy of the check.

"Looks kosher to me," Stone said. "What about you, Dino?"

"If I can keep this I can find out tomorrow if it is real."

"Oh, I know it's real. My attorney checked. After some changes in the offer were negotiated over a period of about ten days, we closed the deal and all the money, two hundred fifty million dollars, was wired to my bank, which gave them a terrible shock. They had never seen anything like it, either. I turned over the business to the new owners and got out."

"That's certainly what I would have done," Dino said.

"I take it you've heard from the buyer more recently."

"How did you know that?"

"Just a hunch. He wants some or all of his money back, doesn't he?"

"The lawyer said that, on taking possession of our plants, the buyer had determined that the air-conditioning and heating in our Massachusetts factory was defective and had to be replaced, at a cost of twenty million dollars."

"How did you respond?"

"I sent him a letter saying that all the heating and air-conditioning equipment had been replaced two years ago, at a cost of eight million dollars. I also pointed out that our contract specified that the buyer had a thirty-day period before closing to inspect the premises and notify us of anything requiring repair or replacement, and that there had been no such notification."

"You've done everything properly, then," Stone said.

"Apparently, that doesn't matter. The lawyer informed me on the phone that his client didn't do business that way, that he preferred informal transactions between honorable men."

"And you said . . . ?"

"I told him that our contract provided that all our dealings would conform to the laws of the State of Massachusetts, and that our dealings were at an end."

"How long ago was this?"

"About a week before you and I met on the sidewalk outside your house."

"And it didn't occur to you to mention all this at that time?"

"I was embarrassed to have become involved with such people, and I was hoping that they would just go away."

"Tell me," Stone said. "What value did you put on the company at the time of the sale?"

"Almost exactly what these people offered me. It occurred to me that they might somehow have gained access to the appraisal letter that was sent to me."

"Have you mentioned this to Mike Freeman or any of the Strategic Services people?"

"No."

"I'll call him in the morning and instruct him to beef up your security."

"Who did you sell the company to?" Dino asked.

"A Delaware corporation, McGlumphy and Whitfield, Inc."

"One created for the purpose," Stone said. "I'll wager they don't have offices or a phone number."

"I've already checked; they don't. Just a P.O. box in Wilmington."

"That's par for the course," Stone said, "and the corporate laws of the State of Delaware are extremely protective of their corporations."

"I've heard that," Shep said.

SIXTEEN

Stone ordered them all a cognac.

"What do you think?" Shep asked.

"I think it's going to go something like this," Stone said. "You'll keep getting demands like this from them, and they'll increase the pressure and the amounts. Finally, they'll want to renegotiate the sale, and they'll make a demand that you can't or won't meet."

"Then what?"

"Then they'll do one of two things: They'll decide you're too much trouble, and they'll go away. Or they'll kill you and go after your estate for the money."

"At what point will it become clear which option they've chosen?"

"That's unclear, but I think it's safe to say that you would be in a hospital for a protracted stay while they're deciding, so neither option is going to be much fun."

"Any suggestions as to my next move?" Shep asked.

"Do you own any real estate other than your father's house in Massachusetts and the Carlyle apartment?"

"Yes, there's a house on Martha's Vineyard. It's nearing the end of a renovation, as we speak."

"Who owns title to the property?"

Shep gave him a small smile. "A Delaware corporation," he said.

"I like it," Stone said. "Is it habitable?"

"Now?"

"Last week would have been better, but I'll settle for now."

"It should be. The builder has asked me to come and approve the finished product. He's worked for us in the past, and he prides himself on finishing on time and on budget."

Stone looked across the room at a couple just being seated. "Just the man I want to see," he said. He stood up and waved, then beckoned.

Mike Freeman excused himself and walked across the room. "Shep, Dino," he said. "Stone, have you got a better idea than my having drinks and dinner with a beautiful woman?"

"Mike, I'm sorry to take you away from all that, but it will only take a couple of minutes to deal with this."

"Let's deal with it then."

"I need to get Shep out of the Carlyle and to a house on the Vineyard at the crack of dawn tomorrow, and he's going to need a detail of at least eight, until this situation is resolved."

"I can deal with all that with one phone call, and you can explain the situation to me later. Shep, a car will pick you up tomorrow morning at six o'clock, *inside* the garage at the Carlyle. Take the service elevator down. You will be transferred to our hangar at Teterboro Airport, and then in our jet to Martha's Vineyard. Do you have a car there?"

"No."

"Then a rental in the name of Strategic Services will be waiting for you, plus a van for hauling my people. We'll talk more after you're settled on the Vineyard. Any questions?"

"No," Shep said.

"Stone? Dino?"

"No," Stone said. "I'll go with him, and I'll get myself to your hangar at Teterboro."

"I'll go with you," Dino said. "This sounds like fun."

Mike went back to his table, and Stone turned over Shep to his Strategic Services detail, who transported him to the Carlyle. "Take a lot of clothes," Stone said. "Do you have any cash on hand?"

"A couple of thousand, in my safe in the apartment."

"I'll bring you some more. For the duration of your stay on the Vineyard, don't use credit cards or write checks, and stay indoors at your property."

"Got it."

"I'll see you at Teterboro at six-thirty AM."

"Good night, Stone, and thanks."

"All part of the service."

S tone waved him off, then turned to Dino. "Pick me up at six AM?"

"Sure."

Stone went home and called Joan from his bedroom. "How much cash do we have in the safe?" he asked.

"Seventy-five grand, give or take."

"Pack twenty-five of it into a briefcase and leave in on my desk. I'm going out of town early tomorrow morning, and I can't tell you where until I'm there. You can text me, if there are problems."

"Okay, boss."

They hung up, and Stone packed two bags.

T he following morning, Stone and Dino arrived at the Strategic Services hangar at Teterboro and loaded their gear into the company's G-500. Shep arrived soon after, and he and a whole bunch of Strategic Services people got on board. They were touching down on Martha's Vineyard less than an hour later, and two vehicles awaited them: a Mercedes S550 sedan and a Mercedes Sprinter, a large van. A half hour later they turned down a tree-lined drive and drove up to a handsome shingle-style house by the sea, maybe five miles from Edgartown.

Stone and Dino were shown to bedrooms while Shep toured the house with the builder, then met the others downstairs.

"Everything is perfect," Shep said, and introduced them to the builder, Mr. Shipley.

"Mr. Shipley," Stone said. "Mr. Troutman is not here and has no plans to be here for the next six months. Please explain that to any of your staff who need to know."

"Right," Shipley said. He shook hands with Shep and left.

"Breakfast?" Shep asked.

"I'm hungry," Stone said.

Shep's cook took their orders and prepared them.

"I've already spoken to the staff about my non-presence here," Shep said. "I trust Shipley and all these people."

"The fewer people you need to trust, the better," Stone said.

L ater, over coffee, Shep looked at Stone and Dino. "Who are we dealing with here?" he asked.

"You mean besides a Delaware corporation?" Stone asked.

"I do."

"Dino, you want to take this one?"

Dino cleared his throat. "Based on my experience with this sort of thing and a little guessing, I think we're dealing with Russians—specifically, the Russian mob."

"Oh, shit," Shep said.

"Well put," Dino replied.

SEVENTEEN

While they were eating breakfast in the kitchen, the Strategic Services detail were moving into the guesthouse and dealing with the electronic facets of the main house.

"What newspapers or magazines do you read?" Shep asked.

"Why?"

"I'll phone the news shop and have them delivered."

"No, no, no," Stone said.

"I don't understand."

"Shep, you have seen that all of us here have gone to great lengths to make you disappear entirely. That means not only that you may not be seen outside this house, but that you cannot contact anyone on the island, like the news shop. You are not here. Understand?"

"I'm sorry to be so thick about this," Shep said.

"Every time you think of someone you want to speak to or someplace you want to go, don't do it. Speak to me or your security detail, and it will be accomplished without your presence or assistance."

"I understand."

"By the way, your phones here have been disconnected, with an order to restore service in six months." He handed Shep a new iPhone, still in the box. "If you need to make a call, use this, after checking with me first. It's registered to a Barbara Harris of Atlanta, who has a part-time residence on the island, so it can't be traced to you or to this house. Give me your old phone."

"What about my phone book and calendar and all that?"

"Already transferred to the new phone."

"Oh."

They exchanged phones.

"The problem, Shep, is that you are a straightforward, honest, and reliable person. You're going to have to begin to be none of those things. Think sneaky."

"I'll do my best."

"One more thing: your detail has placed a FOR SALE sign at the end of your driveway, with a phone number that the detail is managing. Anyone who calls about the house will find it too expensive or uninhabitable or something else to put them off. No one will view the property."

"Good. Stone, will you excuse me for a few minutes?"

"Sure, just don't leave the house or open any doors or windows."

"Right." Shep left the table and disappeared for about twenty minutes, then returned. "Stone, Dino, will you come with me, please?"

"Where to?" Stone asked, rising.

"Not outside. Don't worry." He led them through a large living room and into a walnut-paneled library two stories high, with a spiral staircase leading to a second level. A cheerful fire burned in the fireplace, and a man sat next to it, reading a book. On sighting them, he rose, ready to shake hands. He was tallish, slim, and with an impressive moustache, as white as his hair.

"Stone Barrington, Dino Bacchetti," Shep said, "I'd like you to meet my father, Rodrick Troutman." The older man extended his hand, and they both shook it.

"I'm sorry," Stone said, "I don't . . ."

"Of course you don't," the elder Troutman said. "Call me Rod, everyone does—everyone who knows I'm not dead."

"Are you sure you're not dead?" Dino asked.

"Fairly sure," Rod replied. "Of course, I'm buried under a very nice slab of granite in the backyard."

"No fire," Stone said, pointing at the blaze. "No smoke coming from the chimney."

"It's a gas fire," Rod said. "No smoke. Please sit down, and Shep will explain everything."

Stone and Dino shared a sofa. "Now, do please explain," Stone said.

"I'm sorry to have misled you," Shep said, "but you see, several weeks ago, we began hearing from these people with the Delaware corporation. Dad got tired of dealing with them, so he handed them off to me, and we decided that Dad should be out of the picture. So, with the help of longtime family friends, among them the local chief of police and an undertaker, we simulated Dad's death and removed him here. I'm sorry you missed the funeral, Dad. It was a corker."

Rod laughed heartily. "I'll bet it was."

"So, after it became apparent that the putative buyers were not going to go away, I gently led them down the garden path, separating them from two hundred fifty million dollars of their money. They were foolish enough to think they would get it back. Then my, ah, reoccurring misfortunes began to get in the way, and I came to you, Stone. And you've done exactly what I hoped you would, and flawlessly. Left to my own devices, I would have screwed it up."

"So, Dino, Mike Freeman, and I have had a good look at the garden path, too?"

"You have. What do you think?"

"I think I'll take back what I said about you not being sneaky enough," Stone replied.

"Of course, all your bills will be paid upon presentation," Shep said.

"That's reassuring."

"The City of New York is taking care of me," Dino said. "But you realize I can't stay here past the weekend. I have a day job, down at One Police Plaza."

"Of course."

"How long do you wish me to stay?" Stone asked.

"As long as you like, or as short a time. I think that, after the weekend, we'll be settled in nicely with Mike's people to ward off evildoers."

"Let's look ahead a little," Stone said, "and suppose that whoever these people are, they eventually see through our ruse and come after you."

"Well," Shep said, "in that case we may have to take stronger measures."

Rod spoke up, "I'd welcome the opportunity to shoot a couple of them," he said. "I've got a very nice deer rifle with a big scope on it."

"I don't think a shoot-out is your best move," Stone said. "That sort of thing attracts law enforcement, and you can't buy all the locals and the Massachusetts State Police."

"I've left plenty of room in my backyard cemetery," Rod said.

"Rod, please put that out of your mind."

"All right, then, you're in charge, Stone. What's our next move?"

Dino turned toward Stone. "I want to hear this, too."

"In that case, we will have to discourage them."

"Is that all?" Dino asked. "Just shoo them away?" He made shooing motions with his hands. "How?"

"I'm working on it," Stone said.

Dino laughed. "That means he doesn't have a clue."

EIGHTEEN

R od Troutman stood up. "Perhaps I could show you a couple of things."

"Of course," Stone said, rising in concert with Dino.

"If someone should enter the house without permission," Rod said, walking to a bookcase across the room, "I can take refuge here." He pulled a book—*Tom Sawyer*, from a leather-bound collection of Mark Twain titles—and the entire width of the case, about thirty inches, swung away from him. He ushered them into a bedroom, and the case silently swung shut behind him. Inside were a king-sized bed, a Chesterfield sofa, and a pair of leather reclining chairs. Rod picked up a remote control from a table between them and pressed a button. A very large flat-screen TV rose from a bookcase along the wall and switched on to CNN.

"Entertainment provided for," Rod said, "and there's a shotgun under the bed and a pistol in the bedside drawer. An exit to the outside and two windows are concealed from exterior view." He led the way back into the library and closed the bookcase with another TV remote control next to his chair.

Rod sat back down. "Oh, and there are two turrets at the top of the house, one providing an excellent field of fire toward the road, and another providing the same toward the sea."

"Very well thought out," Stone said.

"Part of the renovation just completed," Shep said, "is armored glass in all the windows. They won't stop a bazooka, but small arms fire can't breach them. There are electric blinds in each, too, so we won't emit light at night."

"I think this house would turn out to be a very unpleasant surprise to your Russian buyers," Stone said.

"I agree," Dino pitched in.

"Still, your best defense is invisibility. If they can't find you, they can't shoot at you. Are there any family members back in Lenox?"

"We are the only two Troutmans extant," Rod said. "I'm thinking of burning down the old place. It's a white elephant, anyway. Nobody in his right mind would buy it, but the land would bring a good price."

"Not just yet," Stone said. "Maybe the Russians will burn it down for you. It's the sort of thing they do."

"And they're welcome to it. I must say, though, Stone, that these people are not going to go away, unless they take some casualties."

"That's an astute observation, Rod, but let's let them start it."

Shep laughed. "I thought they already had," he said, "and I've got the lumps to prove it."

"Still, it's too early to get into a war with these people—and when you do, you'll want to start at the top. They don't care how many soldiers they waste. They'll probably even hide the bodies for you. But it's important to the leaders to feel safe. When they no longer feel that, they'll fade into the forest with the other gnomes."

"Well," Rod said, "I'm told that patience is a virtue, but I've never been all that virtuous. And I'd rather go down while returning fire than be picked off while taking a stroll on the beach."

"An understandable feeling," Stone said, "but we'll all be better off if we can just get them to go away."

"What are you going to do for yourself, Stone?" Shep asked. "You've said you'll go back to New York. They know where to find you, don't they?"

"They do, but I have encountered these people in the past. And, while I can't say that I won, I can say that they felt the pain and didn't like it. Suffice it to say, they don't consider me low-hanging fruit."

"And he's got me watching his back," Dino said. "They know that I'm in a position to make big trouble for them."

"I forgot about the benevolence of the NYPD," Stone said. "My apologies, Dino."

"Accepted."

They had lunch, then Stone went to his room and read for a couple of hours. He was called for dinner at eight. They were on coffee when the team leader of the security detail entered the dining room. "Mr. Barrington," he said, "our Citation M2 will be on the ground in half an hour."

"Then Dino and I had better go and pack," Stone said. "And call my driver." They did so. Then Stone and Dino said their goodbyes and got into the car in the garage. They drove to the main road without lights.

"How do you do that?" Stone asked. "The lights of all modern cars come on at dark, or when the engine's running."

"We have a switch installed that overrides the lighting, inside and out," the driver said.

"I want one of those."

"Mention it to Mike Freeman."

The car switched on its lights at the road. And at the airport, drove onto the ramp. Everything was transferred to the light jet, and the engines started immediately. The pilot already had his clearance, so they were off. Once airborne, Teterboro was half an hour away. When they landed, Fred was waiting with the Bentley, and they dropped Dino off at home.

"The house lights are all off, as you directed, sir," Fred said.

"Good. I don't want to be seen as being at home until after the weekend."

The following morning, Stone called Brooke Alley.

"Good morning."

"Are you still in New York?" Stone asked.

"Yes, are you?"

"Yes, what a happy coincidence. May I give you dinner at my house this evening?"

"You may. Should I bring my toothbrush?"

"Oh, yes."

"Shall I pick up dinner on the way?"

"What do you have in mind?"

"Chinese? From the Evergreen?"

"Sold. You choose the dishes. I'll send my car for you at, say, six-thirty?"

"Done. I'll have the food delivered here."

"See you then."

They both hung up.

Brooke arrived on schedule, and they spread out the food in his study, and they dined on the floor by the fire.

"I called Shep at the Carlyle, looking for you," she said. "They told me he has left the country."

"That's true, sort of," Stone replied.

"Stone, are you hiding something from me?"

"Yes."

"What?"

"Shepherd Troutman. He won't be available for a while."

NINETEEN

The following morning, after they had consumed each other and breakfast, Brooke said, "If you have the time, why don't we chopper out to East Hampton and spend a couple of days at my place there? The weather forecast is good."

"Why not?" Stone asked. "Will we take the service from the East Side heliport?"

"It's my helicopter—or I'm treating it as mine, pending the completed property agreement—but we'll fly from there."

"Do you need to pack?"

"Everything I need is there," she said, "but you can bring as little as you like."

"I'll bring a little, just in case there are unexpected visitors."

"If there are, I'll have security shoot them," she said blithely.

Stone didn't fly helicopters, but he liked the look of Brooke's—cushy leather interior, room for six passengers. As they lifted off, Stone noticed a black chopper at the other side of the heliport, its rotors starting to turn. Crossing the East River, he noticed it seemed to be flying on their route, perhaps half a mile away and slightly behind them. He noted the tail number and memorized it. They flew low along the south coast of Long Island, and the view was increasingly beautiful as they began flying over larger, more expensive houses. He was surprised, three-quarters of an hour later, to find that they were descending. Shortly they alit on a circular spot, surrounded by low boxwoods, with a big H in the middle. "Neatly done," he said to nobody in particular. He gathered up his overnight bag and briefcase and followed Brooke up to a very large, shingle-style house. It made the Troutman place on the Vineyard look modest by comparison.

They crossed a patio and entered the living room, greeted by a white-jacketed houseman who took Stone's light baggage and carried it across the living room to another room, presumably the master bedroom.

"Everything we need is on this floor," Brooke said. "It's the guests who have to climb the stairs or use the elevator, and today, there aren't any."

"Oh, good." There was a table for two set for lunch on the front porch with a pool in the foreground and an unobstructed view across dunes and a beach, of the sea beyond, very blue, since it was a cloudless day.

There were two drinks on the living room coffee table: a glass of champagne and one that turned out to be a Knob Creek on the rocks. "Good choice of bourbon," he said, as she joined him on the sofa.

"I want you to have everything you want, just the way you want it," she said.

"I can live with that," Stone replied.

They lunched on a perfect lobster salad and finished her bottle of champagne. The houseman brought coffee, then she dismissed him, told him to take the remainder of the day off. When they heard the sound of his car driving away, she stood up, dropped the caftan she had been wearing and was naked.

"There's a robe over there," she said, pointing, "if the fire department or anyone else shows up." Stone tossed his clothing to a spot beside the robe, then made himself comfortable in a reclining lounge for two nearby.

"There, isn't that better?" she asked.

"Nudity looks good on you," he said.

"On you, too."

"As long as we aren't interrupted."

"We won't be. I've seen to it." She threw a leg over him and guided him inside her. "There, now we can chat. I'm comfortable, are you?"

"Supremely," he replied.

"Now, tell me about this business with Shep Troutman."

"I'm afraid I can't oblige you: attorney-client confidentiality requires my silence on the subject."

"You're already obliging me," she said, wiggling a little to remind him. "This is just a change of subject."

"It is a subject that is verboten."

"I'll take that as a no."

"Oh, thank you. I'd hoped you would."

"It is not in my nature," she said. "I'm accustomed to hearing all the dirt, and fresh from the mud puddle."

"You're finding other ways to entertain yourself," he said.

"And this is very satisfactory for the bottom end of me, but my ears are empty."

"But not your head. You understand that lives could be endangered, if I were indiscreet."

"I'm the soul of discretion," she replied.

"And I will rely on you to remain so."

"Oh, good. You'll tell me all?"

"I'll tell you nothing, at least, about a client's affairs."

"But you said . . ."

"Discretion is best maintained in the absence of knowledge."

"That seems draconian." She pouted.

"Nevertheless, it is effective." He made a little movement of his own.

"You're distracting me," she said.

"I certainly hope so."

And they put the subject of Shepherd Troutman aside for the moment.

A couple hours later Stone was awakened by the sound of a helicopter passing at low altitude. He raised his head in time to see their earlier shadow flying along the beach at about twenty feet. A man was sitting on the floor, his legs dangling from the open door, a camera with a long lens in his hands. He grabbed a beach towel and threw it over them.

"What?" Brooke said, wakening.

"An unwelcome intrusion," Stone said.

"By whom?"

"That remains to be seen." Stone retrieved his iPhone from his trousers, went online to the FAA website, and entered the tail number he had recognized.

He entered the number into the search engine and waited while it sifted through a long list of aircraft registered in the United States.

Search successful, appeared on the screen.

He clicked on the appropriate spot and received a message on the line below.

The aircraft was registered to McGlumphy and Whitfield. A corporate address appeared below it, then a P.O. box number in Wilmington, Delaware.

"What are you doing?" she asked.

"Looking up the registration of that helicopter," he said. "I had hoped we might get copies of those photographs."

TWENTY

As the sun was setting a little breeze sprang up, and they took shelter in Brooke's caftan and Stone's robe.

"What is your preference for ordered-in pizza?" Brooke asked.

"Domino's medium Extravaganza, hold the green peppers."

"What's on an Extravaganza?"

"Everything, but green peppers."

"What have you got against green peppers?"

"Too green. Also, too herbaceous."

"I like green peppers," she said.

"Okay, just order a medium Extravaganza, and I can pick the peppers off my half. By the way, since I'm naked under this robe, I don't have any pockets, which means I don't have any cash. If you can find my trousers you can rummage through them for my money clip. Tip generously."

She was gone for longer than he thought that would take, then she came back and phoned in the pizza order.

"Did you enjoy reading through the stuff in my wallet?" he asked.

"No, it was mundane: license, pilot's license, insurance card, like that."

"I'm familiar," Stone said. "What did you expect to find?"

"Oh, maybe a picture of a girl, someone to be jealous of."

"God, I'm such a disappointment! I must start carrying more interesting ID!"

"Well, there was that card from the Central Intelligence Agency, identifying you as a special adviser. Are you really in the CIA?"

"No, not really. I'm a special adviser to the director, Lance Cabot. Which reminds me, I need to call him."

"Now?"

"No, not now. Tomorrow maybe, or Monday."

"Why?"

"I can't tell you, since it has to do with that stuff I can't tell you about."

She made a frustrated noise, then went to find a bottle of wine, glasses, and some napkins, tossing Stone a corkscrew. "Will you open it? I can never make these things work."

"Sure. Watch, and you'll know how to do it next time."

He opened the bottle swiftly and tossed the cork to her. "Sniff it to see if it smells good. If it doesn't, we'll open another bottle."

She sniffed it. "It smells good," she said, pouring them each a glass.

The doorbell rang; she answered it and came back with a pizza box. "I tipped him twenty bucks, is that enough?"

"Yes. No wonder he arrived so quickly."

They attacked the pizza. When they were done she asked, "How did you become involved with the CIA. Or, if you tell me, will you have to kill me?"

"That would be the easy way out," he said. "My history with the Agency is long and complicated, and if I explained it all to you, you wouldn't believe most of it. Let's just say that we have found ways to be useful to each other over the years. Besides the card, Lance gave me a badge and a diplomatic passport, which would be helpful in airports, except that I haven't flown commercial in years."

"You have a jet?"

"Yes."

"Me, too—or, as with the houses, I will as soon as the settlement documents are signed."

"You'd better tell Herb Fisher to negotiate the maintenance costs into your agreement. They can be crippling."

"Good idea. When we split, Chet asked me what I wanted, and I said I wanted to go on living exactly the way I have for the

past eleven years, plus a lump sum. He agreed to that, in principle, as you lawyers say, and Herb is making it happen."

"It's a good thing you've got Herb arguing for you, or you'd
be spending the next twenty years in court. When he says, 'Sign
this,' don't hesitate, just do it."

"Herb says I should ask for 'the use' of the jet, not for own-
ing the airplane."

"Smart move. Chet will have to pay all the expenses, as he
always has, so he won't really miss it. If you want to stay on his
good side, give him ample notice of when you want the
airplane."

"I'll remember that."

"What kind of airplane is it?"

"A Gulfstream 700."

"That is a great deal of airplane."

"Chet was good at picking out airplanes and cars."

They watched a movie on the wall-sized TV in the master
bedroom, then fell asleep.

His cell phone woke him. He opened an eye and saw the
sun coming up. A private call. "Hello, Lance," he said,
yawning.

"Don't tell me I woke you."

Stone looked at the bedside clock. "You woke me. What

sensible person wouldn't be asleep at this hour? Hang on a second." Stone got into his robe and walked out onto the deck.

"I hear ocean waves," Lance said. "What shore do they beat against?"

"The south shore of the island called Long."

"Southampton?"

"East, etcetera."

"Your taste in friends is improving. Or have you sprung for some real estate out there?"

"I own too much real estate as it is," Stone said. "Out here, I prefer to mooch."

"Me, too. What were you going to call me about?"

"How did you know I was going to call you?"

"I get these feelings now and then, and you always call."

"Okay, a client of mine named Shepherd Troutman has got himself entangled with what Dino thinks is the Russian mob." Stone related recent events. "And yesterday we were followed from the East Side heliport by a black helicopter." He cited the registration number. "It's registered to McGlumphy and Whitfield, a Delaware corporation, which was also the buyer of Shep's business."

"Where is Shep now?"

"He's holed up on the Vineyard at his father's house. The father is still alive, by the way, but nobody knows it."

"Let me look into it."

"If anybody can bust into a Delaware corporation, Lance, it's you."

"I suppose that's true enough," Lance said. "Talk to you later."

They both hung up, then Stone went back inside, snuggled under the covers again, and went back to sleep.

TWENTY-ONE

Late on Sunday afternoon, Stone packed his change of clothes, picked up his briefcase, and went outside to listen for the arrival of the helicopter. Brooke came and sat beside him.

"Ah, Sunday afternoon," she said. "It's so sad."

"Why is it sad?"

"Because tomorrow is Monday," she said.

"How does Monday differ from any other day for you? You don't have to go to an office, or anywhere else for that matter."

"Yes, but it's still Monday. I used to have to do all those Monday things, and it's sad to remember them."

"If there were no Monday, somebody would have to invent it."

"I suppose."

Stone heard the distant beat of the helicopter's blades. He was about to struggle out of his armchair and walk the dozen steps to the helipad, when the machine appeared from the east. He had expected it from the west, or at the very least, from the south. Then he saw that it was black.

"Do you feel comfortable leaving your house unlocked?" Stone asked Brooke.

"It's locked up tight," she said.

"Never mind, it wouldn't make any difference anyway, if they really want to get inside."

"'They'?"

"Haven't you noticed that it's the wrong helicopter? It's the one that followed us out here."

"Should I call the police?" she asked.

"What, the helicopter police? I don't think East Hampton has one of those." He glared at the chopper. "My kingdom for an RPG," he said.

"What's an 'RPG'?"

"A rocket-propelled grenade."

Then the black chopper peeled off to the east, and Brooke's ex-husband's aircraft appeared from the west and set down on the helipad. Stone and Brooke trotted out to the open door of the machine, Stone ducking, even though he had three or so feet of clearance between his head and the rotors. They boarded, buckled in, and a crewman closed and fastened the door, then they lifted off and turned west, toward the city.

H alf an hour later the towers of Manhattan swam out of the smog and, in what seemed like a moment, they were alighting on the East Side helipad, where the Bentley and Fred awaited.

"Take me home," Brooke said. "I don't think I can stand any more of you."

"That's the nicest thing anyone has said to me all day."

"I mean I'm sore, everywhere that counts, and I don't think I can take any more of you until I've recovered for about a week."

"I'll try and take that as a complement," Stone said. "Fred, drop me off at home, then take Ms. Alley up to Seventy-Third Street and assist her into her residence."

Fred dropped him off, he kissed Brooke and said, "Get better soon."

"God forbid," she replied. "If I call you and invite you over sooner than a week from now, hang up on me."

Stone trotted up his front steps and realized he was pretty sore himself. He went upstairs and sought a nap. He had hardly stretched out when his phone rang.

"Hello?"

"It's Dino. You sound terrible."

"I'm sore," he replied.

"Where?"

"Everywhere that counts."

"That's what happens when you screw in the Hamptons," Dino said.

"How did you know I was in the Hamptons?"

"Because you're sore. Are you well enough to eat?"

"I don't think so. I just laid down, and I don't want to get up again, until at least tomorrow."

"I hear you talked to Lance this weekend."

"Jesus, is there anything you don't know?"

"Not much."

"Did Lance mention how bad everything is?"

"He did. What are you going to do?"

"If I survive until tomorrow, I'll think about it then."

"Sleep with a piece under your pillow." Dino hung up.

Stone fell immediately asleep.

He was awakened by the dumbwaiter bell; breakfast was on the way. He looked at his watch. He had slept straight through the night, a good twelve hours, and he was still sore. He took some aspirin, ate his breakfast, watched *Morning Joe*, then read the *Times* and did the crossword. Afterward he showered, if only to keep from falling asleep again.

As he sat down at his desk, the phone rang. "Hello?"

"I'm feeling better," Brooke said. "Dinner tonight."

Stone hung up and tried to think of something else. The phone rang again, and he picked it up.

"You hung up on me!" she said hotly.

"I was just following instructions."

She thought about that. "Oh."

Stone hung up.

Joan came into his office. "Why do you keep picking up before I can get to it, then hanging up. Is some scam artist pestering you?"

"Something like that."

"Let me deal with it, will you?"

"Okay, you do that."

Joan went back to her office, and the phone rang again. Stone watched the light on the phone; it didn't go out. Joan buzzed him.

"Yes?"

"There's a Brooke Alley on one. Do you wish to speak to her?"

"Yes, but she has instructed me not to take her calls."

"*She* instructed *you* not to answer?"

"That is correct."

"Hang on." She put him on hold.

Stone waited, watching the light on the phone. Joan buzzed.

"Yes?"

"She's on the line, and she says she's canceling her order for you to not speak to her."

"I guess she can do that," Stone said.

"I think she can."

Stone picked up the phone. "You just want to get sore again, don't you?"

"Well, I wouldn't put it quite that way, but you're getting the general idea."

"Tell you what: I'll call you when I'm not sore anymore."

"That seems fair."

"I'm glad you think so. Goodbye." He hung up, then sat staring at the phone. When nothing happened, he went back to work.

TWENTY-TWO

Stone met Dino at Patroon. Dino was half a drink ahead.

"Still sore?" he asked.

"Not so much."

"Have you spoken to Brooke?"

"Several times."

"So why aren't you with her, instead of with me? I hope you're not hoping something will happen between us."

"I have never had that hope and never will."

"You get horny enough . . . well, you never know."

"I know."

"Why haven't the Russians killed you?"

"I don't know. I was half expecting them to try."

"I guess they think there's no point rushing with you, when it's Shep who has their money, and he's not available to kill."

"It wouldn't make any sense to kill him. Then they'd have to deal with his estate, and that could be harder than dealing with him."

"Who's he leaving his money to?"

"I've no idea. He didn't ask me to write a will for him, I assume he already has one."

"Maybe Shep is smarter than we thought."

"His old man, Rod, is smarter."

"Than who?"

"Than any of us. You notice how he waited until he had gotten himself dead before he died? I mean, he set Shep up for this."

"That would presume that Rod knew who he was dealing with," Dino pointed out. "How would an old man who'd lived in western Massachusetts all his life know about the Russian mob?"

"That's an extremely good question, Dino, and I wish I had an answer. It's all very unlikely, isn't it?"

"That's what I was going to say."

"Also, how did the dead hooker get into this?"

"I thought that was one of the cleverest features of this conundrum. Certainly, it was a good way to scare the shit out of Shep, to show him how they had no regard for human life."

"Did you notice that he didn't seem scared?" Stone asked.

"Yes, I did. If I'd been in his shoes, it would have scared the shit out of me."

"Then Shep is a cooler customer than we'd figured," Stone said. "Cooler than I, at least."

"I'll give you that."

"Also, when Mike suggested we get him out of town, and I asked him if he owns real estate outside of the city or Massachusetts, he came up with the Vineyard instantly. And that setup is an extremely complicated set of circumstances."

"Almost too good to be true," Dino said.

"I've never found anything to be too good to be true," Stone said. "Too good to believe, maybe, but not too good to be true."

"I find that all the time," Dino said.

"But you're a cynic."

"I'm a realist."

"No, a cynic is somebody who thinks nothing is good enough to believe, until it's been proved to him two or three times. That's you."

"You're thinking too much," Dino said. "You should give Brooke a call."

"Why are you so interested in my relationship with Brooke?"

"Viv is anxious to know if you're going to have one of those that lasts longer than last night."

"Well, she's just going to have to wait to find out, isn't she? Just as Brooke and I have to wait to find out."

"You're not going to find out by sitting in a restaurant with me, are you?"

"We just need a little time to cool off before we go at it again."

"I've never known you to need a time-out," Dino said. "It worries me a little."

"Don't worry."

"Just a little."

"Not at all. Brooke and I will find each other again quite soon. We agreed to wait until the weekend."

"I guess that's not too much to ask."

"It's proving to be more than I had figured on," Stone said.

"You're not sore anymore?"

"More like itchy. A little. So is Brooke."

"That sounds like the best of all possible worlds," Dino said.

"It ain't bad," Stone said.

Stone's cell phone rang.

"Hello?"

"It's Brooke. Let's have dinner."

"Dino and I are at Patroon. Why don't you join us?"

"Be right there." She hung up.

"Don't tell me," Dino said. "That was Brooke, and she's going to join us."

"How'd you guess?"

"Because she just walked in the door," Dino said, nodding in that direction.

Brooke walked over and slithered out of her fur coat, revealing an elegant black sheath dress with a knockout piece of diamond jewelry at her throat. "Do I have a drink yet?" she asked, shoehorning her way between Stone and Dino.

Stone waved at a waiter, and Brooke asked for a martini.

"Where did you call from?" he asked.

"From the entry vestibule," she replied.

"How did you know where we were?" Dino asked.

"Your wife told me," she replied, taking a big sip of her martini.

"Of course," Dino replied. "I don't know why I asked. Where is she?"

"On a plane to Mumbai," Brooke said.

"Oh, yeah, I forgot."

"May I see a menu, please?" Brooke asked.

A waiter materialized beside her.

"Who'll share the chateaubriand?" she asked.

Both Stone and Dino raised a hand.

"It's a dish for two," she said. "If you like, I'll back out and order something else." She glanced at the menu. "The rack of lamb, please. And a Caesar salad."

"The salad for three, please," Stone said.

It was made tableside, and was quite a performance.

When they had finished dinner and were on coffee and cognac, Brooke said, "I want you now, please."

"To whom were you addressing that request?" Stone asked.

"Would you prefer I address it to Dino?"

"He's a married man."

"That's okay, I'm still a married woman."

"Dino," Stone said, "will you excuse us? I have to get Brooke out of here before she makes a dishonest man of you."

They left.

TWENTY-THREE

It was a footrace to the bedroom, and Brooke won. She was already under the covers, as Stone was hanging up his pants.

"Usually, you just toss them aside," Brooke said. "Am I losing my touch?"

"I don't know," Stone said, crawling into bed. "Touch something." She did. "You're not losing your touch," he confirmed.

Bright and early the following morning, they were eating breakfast. "I have a question," Brooke said.

"Shoot."

"Where is Shep what's-his-name?"

"I haven't the faintest idea about whom you're talking."

"Where is . . . Shepherd Trout?"

"Troutman."

"Okay, Shepherd Troutman."

"What about him?"

"Where is he?"

"Out of pocket," Stone replied.

"That's meaningless. I want a location."

"You mean coordinates? Longitude and latitude?"

"I'm getting the feeling you're not going to tell me where he is."

"You're a very perceptive woman."

"Why won't you tell me where he is?"

"Why do you want to know?"

"I have a girlfriend I want to fix him up with."

"Ah. I'm afraid he's unfixable up at the moment."

"Do I have to guess?"

"You may if you wish."

"If I guess correctly, will you confirm the location?"

"No."

"This is infuriating."

"You're beautiful when you're infuriated," Stone replied.

"Who do I have to fuck to find out where Shep is?"

"Mission accomplished," Stone said.

"Yes, but you haven't told me where he is."

"That is so."

"Will you give him a message to call me?"

"No."

"Why not?"

"Because he might call you."

"Do you object to Shep speaking to me?"

"In principle, no. In practice, yes."

"Who could it hurt, if I put these two people together?"

"Shep."

"Stone, a blind date is not life-threatening."

"You could very well be wrong about that."

"Who wants to kill him?"

"Evil men."

"Why do they want to kill him?"

"For his money."

"Really? Does he have that much money?"

"Yes."

"How much?"

"I can't tell you; attorney-client privilege."

"If you tell me, I'll do exotic things to you."

"You have already done them," Stone replied. "And they were wonderful."

"Would you tell me at gunpoint?"

"Do you have a gun?"

"No."

"Then the question is moot."

"You're talking lawyer-speak."

"I'm a lawyer. It's to be expected."

"What can I do to persuade you to put me in touch with Shep?"

Stone pondered that for a long moment. "I can't think of anything you haven't already done."

"Oh, please."

"You wouldn't respect me, if I told you."

"Yes, I would!"

"If you did, then I wouldn't respect you."

"I'm getting tired of this."

"I was hoping you would."

"You are exasperating!"

"I'm trying to be."

"Well, it's working!"

"Excellent!"

She rolled over and pretended to go to sleep.

"Are you asleep?" he asked.

"Yes."

"What would it take to wake you?"

"Tell me where Shep is."

"Go to sleep."

"I can't sleep."

"Then we'll have to think of something else to do," he said, rolling over.

TWENTY-FOUR

Once at his desk the following morning, after Brooke had taken her leave and been driven home by Fred, Stone called Dino.

"Bacchetti."

"It's Stone."

"And what can your city do for you today?"

"You can put me in touch with your wife."

"She's in Mumbai, used to be Bombay."

"What time is it in Mumbai?"

"I haven't the slightest idea. Whenever I call her in the Far East, I always get it wrong and get yelled at."

"I'll have to risk it, I guess. Where's she staying?"

"At the Taj Mahal Palace."

"Have you got the number?"

"Joan will find it for you."

"I'll call her now."

"Oh, I just remembered she's leaving Mumbai today for Hong Kong."

"What time is her flight?"

"Morning, I think."

"Why don't you know that?" Stone demanded.

"Why would I need to know that?"

"In case you had to call her."

"I've never called my wife in Mumbai."

"Is it morning there now?"

"How would I know?"

"You're being unhelpful."

"I can't tell you what I don't know."

"Well, shit!"

"Why do you want to speak to my wife?"

"None of your business."

"Then why are you bothering me?" Dino hung up.

Stone buzzed Joan.

"Yes, sir?"

"Can you figure out what time it is in Mumbai?"

"It's seven-fifteen PM."

"How do you know that?"

"I just know. Do you want me to place a call for you?"

"Yes, please."

"And to whom do you wish to speak?"

"To Vivian Bacchetti. She's at the Taj Mahal."

"The Taj Mahal is in Agra, not Mumbai, and I don't believe they rent rooms."

"The Taj Mahal Palace Hotel."

"Why didn't you say so?"

"I just did. Call me when she's on the line."

"Yes, sir." Joan hung up and her light on the phone came on.

Stone twiddled his thumbs, until he got tired of that. Joan buzzed.

"Yes?"

"Mrs. Bacchetti is not available. She left Mumbai for Hong Kong."

"How long ago?"

"Twelve hours. Do you want me to call her in Hong Kong? Twelve hours ought to be more than enough to get there."

"Yes, please."

"At what hotel?"

Stone gnashed his teeth. "Call Dino and ask him."

"Yes, sir." Joan's light came on again.

A moment later, Stone's phone rang. "Yes?"

"Stone?"

"Yes?"

"You called?"

"You were going to get me Mrs. Bacchetti, in Hong Kong."

"This *is* Mrs. Bacchetti, and I am in Hong Kong."

"I'm sorry, Viv, I thought you were Joan."

"Was it Joan you wanted to speak to?"

"No, it was you."

"Then speak."

"Of course. Brooke Alley questioned me at some length over breakfast regarding the whereabouts of Shep Troutman."

"Is *that* what you and Brooke do in the early morning? I'm disappointed to hear it. My imagination was more vivid."

"No, we had already . . ."

"Ah, now you're making sense. If you wanted to know where Shep is, why didn't you ask Brooke, if you could get her to hold still for a moment."

"No, the other way around."

"That's always fun, too."

"No, Brooke wanted to know the whereabouts of Shep Troutman."

"Then why didn't you tell her? Why are you calling me in Hong Kong at bedtime?"

"Because I don't want her to know where Shep is."

"Then don't tell her!"

"I didn't. What I want to know is: Why would she want to know where Shep is?"

"Why didn't you ask her?"

"I did, and she said she wanted to fix him up for a blind date with a friend of hers."

"Who's the friend?"

"She didn't say."

"That's unlike Brooke. She always says. Tell me again why you're calling me at bedtime?"

"I want to know why Brooke wants to know how to find Shep."

"How should I know?"

"Well, you know Brooke better than I."

Viv gave a low laugh. "I hardly think so. Now, come on, Stone. What's this about? I'm getting sleepy."

"Why does Brooke want to know where Shep is?"

"I have no fucking idea! Now can I go to bed?"

"All right. Just don't tell Brooke where Shep is."

"I would never tell her. Dino has sworn me to secrecy. Now good night!"

"Good morning," Stone replied.

"What?"

"It's morning here."

"Where are you?"

"In New York."

"Well, it would be, wouldn't it! Good night!!!" She hung up.

Stone reflected on the morning's conversations, at home and abroad. He concluded that they had been fruitless. The only good thing about them was that Brooke still didn't know where Shep was. On the other hand, he still didn't know why she wanted to know Shep's whereabouts.

It was a wash, sort of. He'd have to think of something else.

TWENTY-FIVE

While Stone was still trying to figure out what Brooke wanted, and why, his phone buzzed.

"An anonymous caller for you on line three," Joan said.

"Who is it?" Stone asked.

"It's anonymous. That means he doesn't want you, or maybe me, to know who he is."

"Do we know why he wants to talk to me?"

"He just said you would be interested to hear from him."

"And why is he calling on line three? Isn't that an unpublished number?"

"Yes, but somehow he found it."

"What are my choices here?"

"You can answer it, or I can tell him to go away."

"He could be an important client."

"Yes."

"Or it could be a spam caller."

"Could be. The only way we can know for sure is for you to speak to him."

"Oh, all right." Stone pressed the button for line three. "Hello?"

"Is this Stone Barrington?"

"Who were you trying to call?"

"Stone Barrington. Stone, is that you?"

"That depends on who you are."

"Let me put it this way: I'm calling from an undisclosed location, and I'm trying to be careful, lest I be overheard."

"Do you have a view of the sea?"

"Yes."

"Shep?"

"Yes! I thought you were going to hang up on me."

"I nearly did. How did you get this phone number?"

"I didn't want to call on a line where we might be overheard, and I figured that you had more than one line, and that the numbers were sequential. I called number three."

"Ah! Something this morning finally makes sense."

"Has it been a confusing morning?"

"Don't get me started. How are you, Shep?"

"Very well, thanks. May we talk freely on this line?"

"Yes, we may. Is everything all right where you are?"

"Yes. Well, maybe. The phone here keeps ringing, and I'm afraid to answer it because nobody has the number."

"I have the number."

"Yes, but I was afraid to assume that it was you, so I didn't answer."

"That was a good move, since I didn't call you."

"Should I hang up, then?"

"No, I want to talk to you."

"Is it safe?"

"Yes, the gentlemen from your security firm would have checked out everything."

"Then what do you want to talk to me about?" Shep asked.

"Do you remember Brooke Alley?"

"Man, do I! I still have dreams about that cleavage."

"Can you think of any reason why she should want to contact you?"

"No. Does she want to contact me? Maybe I made the wrong decision when I handed her off to you."

"No, that was a good decision."

"Oh, I'm glad. Things worked out, did they?"

"Sort of. She's been asking where you are."

"For what purpose?"

"I don't know. She wouldn't say. It's possible, of course, that she didn't want to contact you, just that she wanted to know where you were. I thought she might be asking your location at the behest of another party."

"Who?"

"I don't know. That's what doesn't make any sense. Who would she know that wants to know where you are?"

"Beats me," Shep said.

"Do you want her to know where you are?"

"I'll follow your advice on that one, Stone."

"Good. I'd rather she didn't know, so I'll go on refusing to tell her."

"That's fine by me. Unless . . ."

"Unless what?"

"Unless she has, well, ulterior motives. You know what I mean?"

"You mean, she might want to get you in the sack?"

"That's a possible motive," Shep admitted. "It wouldn't be the first time."

"The first time a woman had ulterior motives?"

"Well, yes. After all, you told me that once word got around about my wealth, women would come out of the woodwork."

"Ah, something I forgot: Brooke said that she wants to fix you up with a friend of hers."

"Who?"

"She didn't say. Do you want me to explore this on your behalf?"

"I think that would be a good idea. After all, having been alone with Dad for a while occasionally makes my mind drift to more . . . interesting subjects."

"We'll have to find some way of effecting a meeting without disclosing your location."

"Yes, that could be tricky, no?"

"Yes. I'll call Brooke and feel her out, so to speak."

"Good. Feel her out for me, too, will you?"

"I'll get back to you on this number," Stone said.

"I'll look forward to hearing from you. And Brooke."

"Then I'll see what I can do," Stone said.

They both hung up.

Stone thought about how to handle this and came up dry. He called Dino.

"Bacchetti."

"It's Stone."

"Did you reach my wife?"

"I did."

"Did she send her undying love and affection?"

"No, she didn't. She was a little grumpy."

"About what?"

"She wanted to go to sleep, and I interrupted her attempt."

"One thing you need to know about Viv. If you want something from her, you don't want to piss her off."

"I think that's a policy that should be put into general use where women are concerned."

"Why did you call me?"

"I can't remember."

Dino hung up, and it took Stone a minute to remember why he had called.

TWENTY-SIX

S tone called Brooke.

"Hello?"

"It's Stone. Do you still want to contact Shep?"

"I do."

"Give me your reason again."

"I'd like to fix him up with a girlfriend of mine."

"And what is her name?"

"Why do you want to know?"

"Because Shep is in a high-security situation, and anyone he communicates with has to be investigated first."

"Investigated for what?"

"I can't be specific. Let's just say for nefarious activities."

"Give me an example of a nefarious activity."

"Any activity conducted for nefarious reasons."

"And what does 'nefarious' mean?"

"What it sounds like."

"That's not good enough."

"Then look it up," Stone said. "You have a dictionary on your phone, don't you?"

"Hang on a minute." She came back a moment later. "None of my friends are nefarious."

"We're not talking about your friends as a group, but this one friend that you want to meet Shep."

"She is not nefarious."

"Good. What is her name?"

"I'm not sure I should tell you."

"Then I'm not sure that this conversation shouldn't end right now."

"Oh, all right, it's Phyllis. But she's called Phil, by her friends."

"Surname?"

"You don't need to know that."

"Then I wish you a good day." Stone hung up.

After a count of about eight, Brooke called back. "It's Phyllis Grant."

"Name, address, phone number, Social Security number, and date of birth."

"Why all of that?"

"Because that is the information necessary to run a security check. Cough up or hang up."

Brooke coughed up.

"How is it that you know her Social Security number?"

"Because I figured you might ask me for it," she replied, "and I was right."

"Do you have a street address in Woods Hole, Massachusetts?"

"It's not big enough for street names. Nobody does that."

"Is she married."

"Formerly."

"To whom?"

"Jeffrey Clark, an investment banker."

"Which bank?"

"Goldman Sachs."

"Does she have a roommate, of any gender?"

"She lives alone in a nice little cottage."

"Does she work?"

"She is a painter."

"Does she have a gallery?"

"Yes, in her cottage. It's called, the Grant Gallery."

"Does she sell anyone else's work?"

"No, why should she help the competition?"

Stone couldn't argue with that. "Does she have any connections to Russians?"

"Russians? Like Smirnoff?"

"Or Stolichnaya. People, not vodka."

"Not that I know of."

"All right, someone will be in touch."

"With whom?"

"With Ms. Grant."

"What about me?"

"Is Shep expected to handle you both?"

"I'm not quite sure what you mean by that."

"What are his responsibilities?"

"To be nice, and to pay for dinner."

"And why should you be a party to that? I'm sure Ms. Grant will furnish you with all the details. Good day." Stone hung up. Now how was he going to handle this?

Stone had a thought. He called Mike Freeman's cell phone.

"This is Mike Freeman."

"It's Stone."

"Anything wrong?"

"Not that I know of. I'm trying to get Shep together with a woman for dinner, without blowing his location. Any ideas?"

"Where is the woman?"

"In Woods Hole."

"Well, our mutual yacht is in Edgartown, and I'll call the skipper. A crewman could pick her up, and they could dine aboard."

"Brilliant idea," Stone said.

"We'll run a check on her, right?"

"Right." Stone gave him her particulars. "Thanks so much. I'll wait for news about her."

They hung up.

Five minutes later, Mike called back. "Phyllis Grant is a painter with her own gallery and is divorced from a guy at Goldman. She's clean. No Russian connections."

"Good news. Thank you." Stone called Shep.

"Yes?"

"It's Stone. Got a pencil?"

"Yep."

"Brooke Alley wants to fix you up with a woman." He dictated the phone number. "Her name is Phyllis Grant, known to friends as Phil. She lives in Woods Hole."

"How convenient."

"Easy, you still have to maintain security."

"How do I do that?"

"First, you call the captain of the yacht that I share with Mike Freeman and Charley Fox; she's called *Breeze*, and she's currently berthed in Edgartown. Can your dock take a largish motor yacht?"

"Up to one hundred fifty feet."

"The captain will dock there, you go aboard, and you continue to Woods Hole. While the yacht stands off, a boat is sent to the town dock to pick up Ms. Grant and will deliver her to you. You dine while the yacht cruises up and down Buzzards Bay, then reverse the process. Whatever ensues in between is to be negotiated by the two of you."

"What does she look like?"

"Listen, you're horny enough not to care."

"You're right about that."

"Be sure and frisk her for weapons."

"That would be my pleasure."

They both hung up. "All right, Shep," he said to himself. "Ball's in your court."

S hortly after that, Dino called. "Did you remember what you wanted to talk to me about?"

"I wanted to arrange an assignation, but it's all taken care of now."

"Between you and who?"

"Between Shep and a friend of Brooke's, named Phyllis Grant."

"How are you going to do that without getting him killed?"

"All we have to worry about is that Ms. Grant is not an assassin."

"And how do we know she isn't?"

"Because Mike Freeman checked her out and gave her a clean bill of health."

"Where are they going to meet?"

"She lives in Woods Hole, and *Breeze* is docked nearby, so he'll pick her up, and they'll dine aboard."

"That sounds secure enough."

"We'll soon find out."

TWENTY-SEVEN

S hep noticed that his palms were sweating, and he was a
little short of breath. He dialed the number.

"Hello?"

"Is this Phyllis Grant?"

"Yes."

"This is Shepherd Troutman. Brooke Alley suggested I
call you."

"How very nice. My friends call me Phil."

"And I'm Shep. Would you like to have dinner this evening?"

"I'd love to."

"I'll be aboard a yacht. May I collect you at the town dock at
six o'clock?"

"Can you make it six-thirty?"

"Of course. I'll be aboard a runabout. How will I recognize you?"

"I'll have a rose clenched in my teeth."

"I'll find you. See you then." He hung up, and strangely, he was calmer.

S hep made the arrangements with the captain of *Breeze*, and he was on his dock to be picked up at the appointed hour. The captain welcomed him aboard. "Mr. Troutman, I'm Tim, and we're delighted you're joining us this evening." He led Shep to the fantail, then into the saloon. "Would you like to dine inside or on the fantail?"

"If there's not too much breeze, on the fantail, please."

Tim handed him a card. "This is the chef's proposed menu and wines," he said. "Or you can request anything you like."

"His menu looks good."

Tim gave him a brief tour of the yacht, including the owner's cabin, aft, which had the bed already turned down.

"Do you know Hadley Harbor?" Shep asked.

"Yes, lovely place. We can anchor there for dinner. If you like."

"Just fine."

"I'm told you have some security concerns, so I'll station a couple of crew on the top deck to keep a sharp eye out for intruders."

"Good idea."

They anchored in Hadley Harbor, put the boarding stairs down, and winched down a mahogany tender from the top deck. "A crew member will drive you the short distance to Woods Hole and bring you back here," Tim said.

S hep boarded the handsome tender and took a seat, while the boat sped across the channel to Woods Hole. There was only one woman on the town dock—tall brunette, wearing white trousers, a red-and-white-striped top, and a red jacket. They pulled alongside her. "Phil?"

"Shep?"

"Please come aboard." He assisted her to a seat, then they pulled away from their anchorage. "We're dining in Hadley Harbor," he said.

"How lovely."

M inutes later they were seated on the fantail sofa, ordering drinks.

"Brooke mentioned something about security concerns," Phil said. "What is that about?"

"I did some business with some people who turned out to

be disagreeable," Shep said, "and I don't want to see or hear from them. I hope you don't mind the precautions."

"You mean the man on the top deck with a rifle?"

"I expect so. I'm leaving that to the captain. I understand you're a painter. In what style?"

"Sort of impressionist, I suppose. I paint what I see. And you, Shep. What do you do?"

"I had a career in a family business, and when my father passed on, I sold it."

"To the disagreeable people?"

"They were agreeable enough, until after we had closed, then they began making demands that weren't covered by our contract and I declined to have anything more to do with them. They keep trying to arrange a meeting, one that I have no wish to attend."

"Are you hoping they'll get tired and go away?"

"Exactly."

"And where are you living in the meantime?"

"I left Lenox, in Massachusetts, and moved to New York."

"Where?"

"I have an apartment at the Carlyle Hotel. And you? Are you in Woods Hole the year around?"

"No, I go back to New York in the autumn. I have an apartment in the Dakota, on Central Park West."

"Then you're conveniently located."

She laughed. "I try to be. How long have you had the yacht?"

"Oh, it belongs to some business associates, who were kind enough to lend it to me for our evening."

"I thought you were retired."

"I'm an investor, now." He showed her the menu. "How does this sound? I'm told we can order anything we like."

"Looks good to me. I eat anything."

"So do I."

There was the sound of another boat's engines, and Captain Tim appeared. "Would you mind stepping into the saloon for a moment?" he asked. "We have some passersby who are a little too curious."

They picked up their drinks and stepped into the saloon, where the blinds had been lowered, while the captain stepped out on deck.

"Beautiful boat!" someone yelled.

"Thank you!" Tim yelled back.

"May we come aboard and have a look around?"

"I'm afraid not. The owner does not welcome uninvited guests."

"Is he aboard? May I speak to him?"

"He is at dinner and does not wish to be disturbed."

"Perhaps tomorrow then?"

"Perhaps not, and please keep your distance. We wouldn't want an incident, would we?"

"Whatever you say."

They heard the boat put into gear and begin to motor away.

Tim came back into the saloon. "Perhaps it would be better to serve dinner inside," he said.

"Perhaps so," Shep replied.

"Is that what you've been expecting?" Phil asked.

"I haven't been expecting anything," Shep said. "Least of all, you. You are an unexpected delight."

Dinner was served.

TWENTY-EIGHT

Shep and Phil dined before the saloon's fireplace, which took the chill off the night.

"This is a delightful way to spend the evening," Phil said.

"And you are a delightful person to spend it with," Shep said.

She laughed. "Shep, how long has it been since you spent an evening alone with a woman?"

"Longer than I'd care to think about," Shep replied. "How long since you've had . . . pardon me, dined alone with a man?"

"Your first choice of words would have been appropriate," she replied. "Almost as long as your, ah, abstinence."

"Perhaps we can do something about that after dinner," Shep said.

"I'll think about that," Phil said.

Captain Tim appeared in the saloon with their dessert. "Please let me know when you'd like to go back ashore," he said to Phil. "No rush at all."

"I'd like to go back by midnight," Phil said, then turned to Shep. "I'm in the middle of a painting that I've promised to a client, and I'd like to finish it tomorrow."

"Of course. It's only eight o'clock; we have plenty of time. Shall we have coffee and brandy in the owner's cabin?" Shep asked.

"What a good idea."

Shep gave the steward instructions, and they finished dessert.

The captain came into the saloon. "Your coffee and cognac are waiting in the owner's cabin," he said.

"Any further sign of our visitors?"

"They went past us into the inner harbor, and we haven't seen them since, so I assume they're at anchor there."

"What sort of boat was it?"

"A Hinckley motor yacht, a 43, I should think."

"Did you get her name?"

"No, but a crew caught sight of her hailing port: Wilmington, Delaware."

Shep nodded. "Thank you, Tim. We'll call when we're ready to go ashore."

"Ah, Mr. Troutman, the owners think it would be better if you remain aboard the tender. A crewman will take Ms. Grant ashore and see her to her door."

Shep started to object, but Phil interrupted. "It's all right, Shep. I'll be in good hands."

"Oh, all right. This security business is beginning to get boring."

After dessert, they made their way down to the owner's suite, where they found a silver coffee service and a bottle of cognac with two crystal snifters sitting on a mahogany cart at bedside.

"Oh, how beautiful!" Phil enthused. "Is there a head?"

"One for each of us," Shep said, pointing. "That's yours."

She excused herself, and when she came back fifteen minutes later she was wearing a terry robe. She tossed another on the bed. "I believe this is for you," she said, and busied herself pouring coffee and brandy while he undressed and got into the robe. They drank their coffee sitting up in bed, and then she took away the cups.

"The service is pretty good around here," Shep said.

"And we're only getting started," she said, shedding her robe and tugging at his.

They kissed, and it turned into a long one. Soon, they had

finished their cognac and were naked in bed. From there, things improved—from good to better.

They were asleep in each other's arms when there was a rap on the cabin door.

"Yes?" Shep called out.

"Sir, it's a quarter to twelve. The tender is ready whenever Ms. Grant is."

"She'll be there shortly," Shep said, starting to get dressed.

"You're not coming ashore, are you?" Phil asked.

"I'll accompany you to the town dock, and the crewman can escort you from there."

"Whatever you'd like," she said.

"I'd like to take you home with me," he said. "It's not far."

"Next time."

They shoved off from the boarding ladder a few minutes later and headed into Woods Hole. Shep noticed that there was a Winchester lever-action rifle mounted next to the steering station.

"What's that for?" Shep asked the crewman.

"Pirates," the young man said.

"Do you encounter them often?"

"Well, a boat just followed us out of the inner harbor and is holding back in our wake."

Shep looked back. There was no moon, and it was a cloudy night. He could see nothing.

The crewman hopped out and secured the lines. "I'll be back in ten minutes," he said.

Shep kissed Phil good night and sent her ashore. He collapsed into a chair and pondered for a few minutes what an unexpectedly good evening he had had. Then he sat bolt upright. He heard something that sounded very much like a pistol shot ashore.

Shep grabbed the Winchester, checked to be sure it was loaded, and leapt off the boat onto the dock. He hit the boards running, just as he heard a woman scream and a man shout something.

He remembered from his street map where Phil's house was, and he could see a sign over the door at the end of the street that read: GRANT. As he ran another shot rang out, and the sign shattered and fell in pieces.

Shep looked up. He could have sworn that the shot came from above him. He caught sight of a man leaping from one roof to the next, a gun in his hand. Shep leaned against a brick wall and took aim as the man stood still and looked around.

Shep's first shot spun the man around, then he disappeared below the building's parapet. Shep ran up the street and found

Phil and the crewman huddled in the entry to a shop across the street from hers.

"Back to the boat," he said. "Both of you go ahead, and I'll follow with the rifle." They ran back toward the town dock, while Shep walked back a few yards searching the rooftops for any sign of the shooter. Satisfied that they weren't being followed, he turned and followed them back toward the dock. The engine was running when he leapt aboard.

B ack to *Breeze*," he said to the crewman. "Phil, are you all right?"

"I don't have any holes in me, if that's what you mean," she said.

"That's what I mean. You'll be staying with me tonight."

TWENTY-NINE

For the next two hours they were besieged by half a dozen motorboats and their occupants—various members of the coast guard and two or three police forces. Finally, a uniformed cop with stars on his collar brought them a bloody handkerchief in a plastic bag.

"This is good news," the cop said, holding it up. "It proves you're not crazy. There was a man up there on the roof, but he took the rest of his blood supply with him, and he could be anywhere, asea or ashore, at this point. We'll send it off for a DNA match."

The captain saw the visitors all off the yacht, then came to Shep. "I know you're tired, but I think our best move is to get you to your dock, now, in the middle of the night. The wounded guy is not feeling well, and somebody has to take care of him, and the police have to speak to everyone aboard the Hinckley, so we have a window to escape."

Shep looked at Phil, who nodded. "Right, let's go," she said.

They left Hadley Harbor quietly, at idle speed, then, in deeper water, were headed home at twenty-five knots, with a crew stationed at the radar, watching out for stray boats.

Less than an hour later, they were walking up Shep's dock toward the house, where no light burned.

"Nobody home," Phil said.

"My dad is there," Shep replied.

"I thought he was dead?"

"Not really. We just want the world to think so. Me, too, for that matter."

They came to the back porch, and as Shep was tapping in the security code, a flashlight suddenly played over then.

"State your name and business," a deep voice said, over the sound of a shotgun being racked.

"I'm Shepherd Troutman, and the lady is Ms. Grant, my guest.

"Good evening, Mr. Troutman. Miss. We thought you were sleeping aboard."

"I'll tell you about our evening in the morning," Shep said, "but right now, we're very tired."

"Of course, go right in, sir."

S hep took Phil upstairs to the master suite and showed her to her dressing room and bath. "Would you like a nightshirt to sleep in?"

"I never sleep in anything," she said.

That turned out to be true, except in his arms.

T he following morning they had breakfast in bed. "Do you have a friend in Woods Hole who can get into your house?" Shep asked.

"A woman comes daily to run the shop, while I paint."

"Why don't you call her, ask her to pack a bag or two for you and to FedEx them here. You'll have them tomorrow."

"Good idea."

"Tell her to be cautious, not to let anyone have a look at where they're going."

"She's very discreet," Phil said.

"Use line three on the phone. I have to go talk to the security people." He went downstairs and found their leader in the kitchen, drinking coffee, and told him of their experience of the previous night.

"You'd better not use the yacht again," the man said. "If you need water transport, we'll provide it."

"Ms. Grant is going to stay for a few days, and she's asking a friend to FedEx her some clothes."

"We'll have a man at the FedEx office to receive them and bring them back by a circuitous route."

"Excellent." Shep went to his study and called New York.

"The Barrington Practice," Joan said.

"It's Shep Troutman, Joan," he said. "May I speak to Stone?"

"Of course."

Stone came on the line. "Good morning. Everything okay?"

"Yes, but it wasn't so last night." He related the events as they had occurred. "I suppose I didn't handle it well. Somebody spotted me."

"I think you handled it as well as it could be handled," Stone said. "You got out of there, and they can't know where you went."

"Not unless they knew where I came from," Shep said.

"I would discount that theory. Is it all right if I come up and stay for a night or two?"

"We'd be glad to have you for as long as you like. Bring company, if you so desire. Phyllis Grant turned out well. You'd think she got shot at all the time."

"Good. Don't either of you leave the house before I get there. We'll need to rethink your security."

"All right. Do you want to be met at the airport?"

"I'll get myself to the house. Safer."

"As you wish."

"I'll bring Dino, too, if he can shake loose."

"Sure." They both hung up.

S tone called Dino.

"Bacchetti."

"A little kerfuffle north of here," Stone said.

"How little?"

"Could have been a lot worse, but nobody on our team got hurt. I'm going back up there for a couple of days. You game?"

"Sure. It's boring here."

"Pick me up in your car, and your driver can take us to the airport. Bring sporty clothes. We'll want to blend in."

"Okay."

"Two o'clock?"

"Good." They both hung up.

T he Strategic Service Citation M2 set down at mid-afternoon.

"Did you book a rent-a-car?" Dino asked.

"No."

"Are we hitchhiking?"

Stone pointed to a photograph of two tourists on Vespas.

"Like that."

"I haven't been on one of those things since high school," Dino said.

"You've been on a police motorcycle or two," Stone said. "It's like roller-skating or sex. You never forget how."

"I hope you're right," Dino said, "for the sake of my bones."

Their bones made it all right. They stopped at the front gate of the house, took a leak, and tried to look like tourists. Finally, they drove to and around the house and parked in a shed at the rear.

Shep came down the back stairs to meet them. "Sorry, no tourists allowed," he said.

"Make an exception," Dino replied.

"Come inside."

THIRTY

Stone and Dino sat in the library with Shep, Phil, and two of the security detail, listening once again to Shep's account of the events of the night before. Stone was very impressed with how calmly Shep and Phil had handled themselves after the rude shock of having been shot at.

"Did anybody get the name of the Hinckley boat?"

"No," Shep said. "And the captain stressed that it wasn't necessarily the Hinckley model 43, that was just an approximate length."

"Pity about not having the boat's name," Dino said.

"Oh," Shep said. "One of the crew got the Hinckley's hailing port: it was Wilmington, Delaware."

Stone and Dino exchanged a glance.

"Ah, I get it," Shep said. "Our purchaser was a Delaware corporation."

"Correct," Stone said. "Tell me," he said to the security people, "are there any very large yachts moored in Edgartown?"

"I don't know," the woman said, "but I can call the harbormaster and find out. Why do you want to know?"

"Because a Hinckley 43 is a nice boat—I own one—but it's not nice enough to massage the ego of the kind of person we're dealing with. It could, however, be a tender to a very large yacht."

"A forty-three-foot tender?" Shep said.

"If your yacht is one hundred fifty feet, that would make perfect sense," Stone said. "You'd sometimes have a lot of guests, and there would be a lot of work for a boat of forty-three feet to do. They might even have a pair. What color was the hull of the Hinckley?"

"Dark—blue or black."

The security agent excused herself, then came back after a few minutes. "A two-hundred-footer came in yesterday morning," she said. "She was too big for the available space in the marina, so she's anchored across the harbor. Her name is *Nostrovia*, which is an English misspelling of a Russian name I can't even spell: it's a toast—literally, 'Let's get drunk.'"

"Ah," Stone said.

"Oh, and she has two tenders, both Hinckley 43s, dark blue."

"Well," Dino said. "Now we know who we're dealing with."

"What's the length of *Breeze*, Stone?" Shep asked.

"One hundred twenty-five feet," Stone replied.

"Let's sink the Russian," Dino said, and everybody laughed.

"You'd need a torpedo or two, Dino," Stone said, "and a submarine to fire them from."

"It was just a thought," Dino said.

E verybody was tired, and they went to bed early. Stone was lying in bed, on the edge of sleep, when there was a soft knock at his door. "Yes?"

The door opened, Phil walked into the room, clad in what Stone suspected was only a terry robe, and sat on the edge of his bed. "You're not asleep yet," she said. "Is there anything I can do to help?"

Stone sat up. "And whose idea was that?"

"Mine," she said. "Shep is a heavy sleeper, and I'm not. Have I offended you?"

"Not in the least," Stone said, "but together, we might offend our host. However, you've given me an idea." He picked up his cell phone and called a number, which was quickly answered. "Hello, there," Stone said.

"What a nice surprise," Brooke said.

"Are you up for a little travel tomorrow?"

"Where?"

"I can't tell you that, but you'll know when you arrive. Can you drive a Vespa?"

"I owned one in college."

"Okay, here's how it goes: Fred will pick you up tomorrow morning and drive you to Teterboro, then into a large hangar, where there will be a light jet called a Citation M2. You will board that and be flown for less than an hour. When you land, there will be a Vespa reserved for you. Write down these directions." He gave her instructions on finding the house. "There will be a sign saying 'private' on the front gate. Don't stop. Continue down the road to the village, make a few turns to make it difficult to be followed; narrow streets are best. Then drive out of town, back to the house, then around the house, and park in the shed with the other scooters and scratch at the back door of the house."

"What clothes shall I bring?"

"Beachy, country clothes. You won't need a ball gown. If Fred picks you up at ten, you'll be here for lunch."

"Got it!" she said.

"Sweet dreams." They both hung up.

"I think that's a better solution to my problem," Stone said.

"I'm disappointed, but I can't deny that."

"Go make Shep happy," he said, and she left, closing the door softly behind her.

THIRTY-ONE

S tone was in the study, reading the *Times*, shortly before noon, when he heard the *putt-putt* of a Vespa driving around the house to the rear. He put his paper down and went out back to meet Brooke.

"You made it," he said. "Welcome! Did you have a good trip?"

"Pretty good for a girl who had no idea where she was going," Brooke said, unbuckling her helmet and freeing her bag from its bonds on the luggage rack. "I thought it was going to be Bermuda, at first."

Stone took the bag and felt the weight of it. "No ball gown?"

"Nope; I'll fit right in. If we need it, you can supply some hayseed for my hair."

"You'll do fine, after you've brushed out the imprint of the helmet on your hair."

She shook her head like a dog. "How's that?"

"Just fine." He explained who the other people in the house were going to be, then he took her to their room and left her to freshen up. "Lunch is at twelve-thirty, drinks at six-thirty, dinner at seven-thirty."

"And breakfast?"

"In bed, as always."

"Oh, good."

He went back to the study and resumed his reading of the newspaper.

They gathered for lunch in the kitchen, where the cook, Melba, called 'Cook,' specialized in good, solid New England comfort food. Today's was cod.

When they were on coffee, Doug, the security team leader said, "Let me give you a status report."

They all settled in.

"I had worried that, after the shootout of the night before last, we might have blown our cover and had to move. We still might have to, if something else like that occurs."

"Wait a minute," Brooke said. "'Shootout'?"

"I'll bring you up to date after lunch," Stone said. "Let Doug continue."

"I didn't bring my vest and combat gear," she said.

"You won't need it, Brooke," Doug said. "We're secure here, as of this moment."

"I'm glad to hear it."

"We've kept a watch on radio traffic," Doug continued, "aviation, nautical, and even CB. And we've not heard a discouraging word. Stone, your yacht captain and his crew are to be complimented for the way they handled an unexpected situation. However, the opposition is aware of *Breeze*, now, so all of you should stay away from her, unless we use her as an escape vessel, and that would be in the middle of the night."

"Doug, do you think we should have a look at *Nostrovia*?" Stone asked.

"We already have, from the air." He took photos from an envelope and passed them around the table. "As you can see, there are a number of places where weapons could be mounted, and a helipad, but no chopper present. It's hard to see anything of a vessel of that size from the water; all you can see is the wall of her hull, which is steel." He pointed to the upper deck. "You can see one of the Hinckley 43s here. And Stone was right. They're not too large for tenders on a ship of that length."

"Do they have an airplane at the airport?"

"We've run all the tail numbers of the aircraft out there and have come up with nothing—a Delaware registration, for instance. I suspect that something flew them in, then got out. I'm sure it will be available, if they choose to depart in a hurry."

"How many crew aboard, do you think?" Stone asked.

"At least twenty, possibly more. Two of them went ashore for groceries this morning. They all wear white trousers and navy blue polo shirts, with the yacht's name embroidered on the chest. It makes them easy to spot."

"Or hard to spot," Stone said, "if they change into civvies."

"Good point. That's all I've got, for the moment," Doug said.

"Good report, Doug," Dino said. "If you ever want to join the NYPD, give me a call."

"Thanks, I'll keep that in mind, Dino, if I fall on hard times."

"What's your definition of 'hard times,' Doug?" Shep asked.

"A job that pays less than Strategic Services."

"Have we had any flyovers here?" Stone asked.

"Not a one. I'd expected a chopper, and we might see one yet, if they get bored looking for us around the island. But from the air, we look like a house closed for the off-season."

Lunch broke up. "Is there somewhere I can get some sun?" Brooke asked Doug.

"Not unless we need bait," Doug said. "The sight of you lying around in a bikini, or less, could attract a lot of attention."

"Thank you, Doug," she said, batting her eyes rapidly.

"Do we have a sun lamp in the house?" Stone asked Shep.

"I'm afraid not. Normally, sunshine is abundant around here, but the circumstances . . ."

"Don't worry about it," Brooke said.

"There's a large library, if you'd like to read something."

"I'd like to do the *Times* crossword, please."

"There are three copies of the paper lying about," Stone said. "I'll find us both one."

They repaired to the library for an afternoon of reading and television. They had been there for a couple of hours when they heard the sound of an airplane flying over, followed by a loud noise from outside.

Shep came trotting into the library. "We're being bombed," he said.

A voice came over the house-wide sound system. "Nobody go outside!" Doug commanded. "Continue as you were, and stay away from the windows."

"What the hell?" Dino asked.

"Beats me," Stone said. "Let's do as Doug says."

After a few minutes, Doug came into the library. "An airplane has dropped a bomblike object on the shed where the scooters are parked," he said. "One of our team is an old bomb-squad guy from the military, and he will be checking it out in due course. In the meantime, stay out of the kitchen, which is the room with the most exposure."

After another hour, Doug came back and said, "Come with me to the kitchen." They followed him and had a look at an object about eighteen inches in length, which looked like a bomb. "It's not a bomb," Doug said. "It's a harmless fake, used in the military to simulate bombings. I think they dropped it on the shed to see if we would all run out to see what happened, but we didn't rise to the bait, so we're fine."

"They must be conducting a search up and down the beach, looking for us. This doesn't mean they've found us."

THIRTY-TWO

Stone and Brooke had worn themselves out after breakfast, when there was a knock at the door, and an envelope was slid under it. Stone retrieved it and found it addressed to himself.

"This was in the mailbox this morning," a woman's voice said from the other side of the door.

Stone got back into bed and examined the envelope closely. It was made of expensive paper, and the handwriting of his name was in a florid script. There was no stamp on the envelope.

"Aren't you going to open it?" Brooke asked.

"I'm not even here. Why am I getting mail?"

"I don't think we're going to find out by not opening it."

"Oh, all right." Stone opened the envelope and shook out a single sheet of notepaper. At its head was one word: *Nostrovia.* He read the handwritten note.

> *My dear Mr. Barrington,*
>
> *I would be very pleased if you and your guests*
> *would join me aboard my yacht for cocktails. Dress*
> *is informal, and my tender will be ready to depart*
> *the yacht club at six o'clock.*
>
> *Gregor Kronk*

"Well, that's bold," Stone said. He got dressed and went to find Doug, who was working at the kitchen table. Stone handed him the note. "What do you think of that?"

Doug read it again. "He's feeling us out," he replied. "He doesn't know how many of us there are and who we are."

"Should we go?" Stone asked.

"It would be a good opportunity for us to help him underestimate us."

"How do you mean?"

"Well, we're fourteen here. Suppose you and I and the two ladies, and one other of my team, attend. Here's our story. The late Rod Troutman was a good friend of yours, and you had made it a practice for several years to visit him here at this time. This year you got a note from the office of his estate, saying that

175

the invitation was open, as usual. So, you invited two other couples to join you. You can say that you suspect that the estate would like to sell you the house."

"I like it," Stone said. "We don't have to lie too much."

"The simplest lies are the best ones."

"We'll take three scooters to the yacht club, and we'll take a few other items, as well."

"What items?"

"Bugs. Gregor Kronk has handed us an invitation to wire his yacht."

Shortly before six o'clock they were met by a Hinckley tender at the yacht club and ferried to the mooring of *Nostrovia*. The boarding stairs rose only halfway up the hull, then they stepped inside and were taken in an elevator to the main deck.

They emerged into a large saloon, with a big fireplace at one end. A large, powerful-looking man in a double-breasted blue blazer and white trousers greeted them. "Mr. Barrington?" he said, approaching Doug.

"No, this gentleman is Mr. Barrington," Doug said, indicating Stone.

"Ah, my apologies." He offered his hand, and Stone shook it.

"Not at all, Mr. Kronk, and thank you for your invitation. We had seen your yacht in the harbor and were curious about it. I think it must be the largest vessel to be seen in these parts since the days of Aristotle Onassis and his *Christina*."

"Perhaps so. Is Mr. Troutman not with you?"

"I'm sorry, Rod Troutman passed away some weeks ago. I had visited him here at this time in previous years, and his estate invited me to come again. I suspect they would like to sell me the house."

"I'm surprised you are not aboard your own yacht. *Breeze*, I think she is called."

"She is, but I have two partners in the yacht, and one of them is using her at this time. They departed this morning, I believe."

"And where is young Mr. Troutman, Shepherd?"

"I last saw him in New York, but he had an unpleasant experience there, and left town. I don't know where to."

"I heard he had bought a very nice apartment at the Carlyle."

"You are very well informed, Mr. Kronk."

"I try."

"After his experience, he canceled the purchase of the apartment and moved out. I'm not sure where."

"You don't keep track of your clients, then?"

"We know where to send their bills," Stone said. "Otherwise, no."

"May I show you around *Nostrovia*?" Kronk asked.

"Yes, please. We'd love to see her."

Kronk led the way from stem to stern, with a running commentary on its furnishings, which were excessively opulent.

"When are you returning to New York?" Kronk asked.

"Oh, in a day or two, as soon as the ladies start to get bored."

"And how did you arrive?"

"My friends use an air charter service. I was visiting other friends on the Cape, and I and Ms. Alley met *Breeze* at Woods Hole and were conveyed by her to the house."

"How convenient."

"We found it so."

"Will you stay aboard for dinner?" Kronk asked.

"That would be lovely, but I'm afraid we are otherwise engaged."

"Perhaps another time," Kronk said.

"I do hope so."

In due course they were returned to the tender, and thence to the yacht club. As they climbed onto the dock, Doug held a finger to his lips. When they were back at the scooters, he turned up Stone's jacket collar and produced a bug.

"It appears that Kronk was like-minded," he whispered, slipping it into a metallic envelope and pocketing it.

"How many did you plant aboard *Nostrovia*?" Stone asked.

"Only a dozen. I wish I had brought fifty, but that was all I had."

"Well, twelve will give us something to listen to," Stone said.

"I thought your story was very good," Doug said.

"It was close enough to the truth to confuse him, I hope. He must have been surprised to hear that his people were shooting at me, instead of Shep."

"We must continue to confuse him at every turn," Doug said. "We can use his own bug for that purpose." He searched everyone else for bugs, but found none.

THIRTY-THREE

They dined on a discussion of *Nostrovia*. "Some of the furnishings were ornate to the point of being grotesque," Stone said.

"She was a perfect example of the owner who has too much money and not enough to spend it on," Brooke chimed in.

"Do you think Kronk will stop chasing us now?" Shep asked.

"Perhaps," Stone said. "Let's see if he believed my story of your departure to parts unknown."

Brookes spoke up, "I've never understood why all this is happening," she said.

"Neither had I," Shep said, "until this afternoon."

"Enlighten us," Stone said.

"I remembered something, and I'll have to check it out: I

think it may be the result of Mr. Kronk's attorneys not reading the sales documents thoroughly."

"Oh, good. I love lawyers' mistakes. What's this one?"

"We have a machine that we have developed over three generations, and its patent was withheld from the sale. Perhaps they didn't notice. Odd, because it's probably the most valuable of the company's possessions."

"What is the machine?"

"We call it a multilathe, though the name is an oversimplification. It's a very complex piece of equipment that can create a large number of machine parts at once, each to a very precise specification. We used to sell the parts to our customers, but in the past few years we decided that it was better to license the patent and let them make their own parts, but at a very high price. It's a huge income producer for the company. I believe that Kronk has discovered the error and is trying to get the patent without paying for it, and thinks that would be easier with me out of the way. The patent is probably worth more than the company."

"If you were selling it to him what price would you put on it?"

"Perhaps half a billion dollars, or even more."

"More," Rod Troutman said.

"Ah," said Stone. "Does Kronk think you have cheated him?"

"I shouldn't think so, because his attorneys wrote the contract."

"And they've probably been taken out and shot by now," Dino said.

"So all this is over a machine?"

Shep shook his head. "No, it's over a piece of paper: the patent on the machine. We licensed the patent to ourselves some years back, and the license is coming up for renewal quite soon."

"Have Kronk or his attorneys asked for the patent?"

"No, but I expect they'll get around to it," Shep replied. "If they've noticed the omission from the contract."

Rod Troutman began to laugh.

"What's so funny, Dad?"

"This whole business. It's hilarious! I love doing this to these people!"

"Shep," Stone said, "where is the actual, physical patent now?"

"In the company safe, in Dad's old office," Shep said.

"So, it's obtainable?"

"If they haven't changed the combination," he replied.

Rod spoke up. "I doubt if they could open it, even if they have the combination. It's a very special safe."

"What kind of safe?"

"An Excelsior. It was made in Berlin shortly before the outbreak of World War II, and the factory was bombed to dust during that misunderstanding and the owner killed. My father ordered the safe on a trip to that city, and it was shipped, I believe, in June of 1939. They sent a technician with it to see that it was properly installed and that the new owners could open it."

"If the combination has not been changed," Stone asked, "could you open the safe?"

"The last time I tried, it took three efforts before I got it right," Rod said.

"Were you present when the safe was delivered in 1939?" Stone asked.

"Yes. I was a small boy, of course, but the safe fascinated me. I remember that the technician lectured my father firmly about keeping me away from the safe, so I wouldn't get locked in."

"Do you remember the man who installed it?"

"I do, oddly enough. He was an impressive man—tall, ramrod straight, with a handlebar moustache. He had a name that amused me, but for the life of me, I can't remember it right now."

"Could his name have been Solomon Fink?" Stone asked.

Rod's face lit up. "Yes! How on earth could you know that?"

"We've met, he and I."

"My God, he would have to be more than a hundred years old!" Rod said.

"A hundred and five, now, I think."

"How did you know him?"

"A very good friend of mine—Dino's father-in-law, Eduardo Bianchi—died last year. When his daughter—Dino's ex—was clearing out his study, they found a safe concealed behind a bookcase. An Excelsior. No one had the combination; apparently, Eduardo had taken it to his grave."

"Did you ever get it opened?"

"Yes. A business associate of mine said that he knew a very talented safecracker, who might be able to open it. His name was Solomon Fink, and he was resident at a very nice nursing home in Brooklyn. He was a hundred and four years old. As it turned out, he had installed the safe, apparently, on the same trip when he installed the one in your father's office, Rod. Wisely, he never went back to Berlin."

"Could he still remember the combination?"

"Yes, but as it turned out, he didn't need it."

"Why not? How could he open it without the combination?"

"I watched him do it. He bent over, ran a finger along the bottom of the safe's door, and pulled off a piece of tape. The combination was written on it. He opened the door in seconds."

"Do you think there might be a piece of tape on my father's safe?"

"There might be."

"Well, Dad," Shep said. "How on earth do we find out?"

"I suppose we'll just have to break into my old office," Rod said.

"Do you still have the keys?"

"I have the keys to every door in the building," Rod replied.

"Do you still have the combination?" Stone asked.

"It's in my head," Rod said, "and thus, may or may not be accessible."

"Then we'll just consult the strip of tape on the bottom of the safe's door."

"How do we know it's there?" Shep asked.

"I'll call Sol Fink and ask him," Stone replied.

THIRTY-FOUR

S tone checked his iPhone contacts and touched the
number.

A woman answered. "East River House," she said.

"May I please speak to Mr. Solomon Fink?" Oh, God, he
thought, what if he's dead?

"He should just be finishing dinner," she said. "Let me see
if I can connect you with the library. He usually has coffee and
brandy in there. Please hold."

Alive! And drinking coffee and brandy! "I'll hold."

He held, and a deep voice said, "This is Solomon Fink."

"Sol, this is Stone Barrington. How are you?"

"Stone! It's good to hear from you. Are you in New York?"

"No, I'm in another location, one I can't disclose for business
reasons."

"No need for me to know, is there?"

"I suppose not. I have a question for you, Sol."

"Shoot!"

"Do you recall installing an Excelsior at Troutman Industries, a factory in Lenox, Massachusets, in . . ."

"June of 1939," Sol said. "Of course. I installed that one of your friend Bianchi's on that same trip, then I managed to forget to go back to Germany."

"That's the one. Do you recall if you taped the combination somewhere in the room where the safe was when you were done?"

"That was my normal practice, but I can't say for certain if I did so on that occasion. Do you want to open it?"

"Yes. Two of Mr. Troutman's descendants are my clients."

"Do they have the combination?"

"Mr. Rod Troutman memorized it, but isn't sure if he can recall it on demand."

"Then I'll have to make another trip to Massachusetts, I suppose."

"Do you feel up to the trip, Sol?"

"I do. How long a drive is it?"

"Oh, we'll fly you up in a private jet."

"Wonderful! I've never flown in a private jet."

"You'll enjoy the experience."

"When?"

"I'll need to talk to the Troutmans and make some arrangements. May I phone you back in a day or two?"

"Of course. This is a good time of day."

"I'll speak to you then," Stone said, and they both hung up. Stone went back to the dining room. "Good news: Solomon Fink is alive and well and says he'll come to Massachusetts to open the safe, if necessary."

"I may be able to remember the combination," Rod said, "but did you ask if he had concealed it somewhere?"

"I did, but he's not sure. And, Rod, unless you're certain you have the right combination, you shouldn't try to open it. If you enter the wrong combination too many times, the beast will lock you out. Then there's nobody in the world to open it but Solomon Fink."

"Perhaps we should invite him for a visit, then."

"I have already done so, and he has accepted. My concern now is access to the safe. You say you have all the keys?"

"I do."

"Then we will have to find a way to get past whatever security arrangements the new owners have made."

"I still have friends there," Shep said. "I can find out what they've done."

"We'll need passcodes, too, and the knowledge of security guards, if any, on the grounds and in the building."

"I'll make a couple of phone calls," Shep said.

"I'll do it," Rod interjected.

"You can't call anybody, Dad. You're dead, remember?"

"Ah, yes. Slipped my mind."

"Rod," Stone said, "why don't you write down the combination that's in your head. It may come in useful."

"Of course," Rod said. He was handed a pad and pen.

"Write it down three times, Dad," Shep said.

Rod grasped the pen, wrote it down, ripped off a page and wrote it a second and third time.

Shep looked at the three pages. "That's great, Dad, thanks." He put the sheets in his pocket.

They were served coffee and brandy in the library.

"Shep," Stone said, "you look concerned."

"I think you'd better get Mr. Fink up to Lenox as soon as you can. When do you want to go into the factory?"

"Are your employees churchgoing people?" Stone asked.

"Most of them. Why do you ask?"

"How about Sunday morning?"

"Perfect. The heathens will be on the golf course."

"Good. Would you still definitely like to bring up Sol Fink?"

"Yes. Because Dad wrote down three different combinations."

"Oh."

THIRTY-FIVE

S tone walked into Rod's study later that night. Shep was at the desk, making phone calls.

"How's it going?" Stone asked.

"It's going. The good news is, the new owners haven't done anything radical to the security system, which we installed a couple of years ago. The entry codes have changed, but I have them in my notebook."

"Is the safe still in your dad's old office?"

"Yes, and they haven't been able to open it."

"We're going to need Sol on site, then."

"Yes. One thing: they're bringing a safecracker up from New York on Monday, and they expect he'll open it."

"Is Rod's office occupied by someone new?"

"Yes, a man named Mueller, a German national whose job

it is to visit their new acquisitions and get rid of the fat on the payroll. As you can imagine, he's not very popular; behind his back they call him the führer. He plays golf on Sunday mornings."

"What else is in the safe, besides the patents?"

"I don't remember. It's been a long time since I was inside it."

"We'll have to bring Sol up on Saturday and accommodate him somewhere that night."

"Right. He will fly into the Pittsfield Airport."

"Where can we stash Sol for the night?"

"At Dad's house. We keep a skeleton staff there to tend to it, and I'll have them bring in anyone that's necessary, like a cook. It's a big place. We can all stay there."

"Are we going to drive?"

"That would involve a ferry going and returning, with a long drive in between. Why don't we have your airplane land here and pick us up, with Sol already on board, and fly us to Lenox? I can have us met there."

"Good idea. I'll arrange the flight while you deal with the domestic arrangements."

"How many will we be?"

"You and I, Sol, and Doug, for security. I'll speak to him about it." Stone left and went looking for Doug. He found him in the kitchen, having just finished his rounds.

"A word, Doug?"

Doug waved him to a chair at the kitchen table. "What can I do for you, Stone?"

"Four of us, including you, are going to make a little excursion tomorrow."

Doug's eyebrows went up. "What kind of excursion?"

"A Citation M2 is going to pick us up tomorrow and fly us to Lenox, Massachusetts, for an overnight stay."

"Why?"

"We need to retrieve some documents from an old safe in Rod's former office. We'll do it on Sunday morning, when everybody at the factory is either in church or on the golf course."

"You want me to arrange accommodations?"

"Already done. We'll be staying at Rod's house. Shep is arranging for a cook and other staff."

"How are we planning to get into the factory?"

"Rod has all the keys."

"Is Rod going with us?"

"No, he's still dead, and we don't want him spotted in the neighborhood."

"How are you going to get into the safe?"

"We have an expert joining us. We'll be back here by noon on Sunday, then the airplane will take our yegg back to Teterboro."

"Okay, let's sum up," Doug said. "You're going to take a man we've gone to a great deal of trouble to make disappear, and land him in the middle of an area where he's well known; then we're going to get ourselves into a building where we have no information on the security system, get into a safe, steal the documents, get back to the airport, and fly back here, right?"

"Well, we're reliably informed that the security system hasn't been altered, except for new entry codes, and we have those."

"That's a relief, but nothing else you've told me is. This is going to be a terribly insecure mission."

"Please tell me how we can make it more secure."

"I'm going to need six more people, and none of them from this house. They can meet us there. They'll need to be licensed to carry in Massachusetts. I'll need to arrange transport from the airport to the house, and . . ."

"Shep is arranging that."

"What, in the family limo, which will be well known in those parts? Or is he renting, using his own credit card?"

"All right, Doug. Sketch out a plan and brief us all."

"I'll have something for you to look at later tonight. Does Rod or Shep have any plans of the house or the factory? Or even just photographs?"

"I'll ask."

"Please. Oh, and Stone?"

"Yes?"

"You're going to need a bigger airplane, so our people can fly up with your yegg."

"I've got a Gulfstream 500."

"That'll do."

Stone went looking for Shep, but first called Joan and asked her to arrange Fred and the Bentley to pick up Sol at the home, then take him to Teterboro, then get Faith, his pilot, to arrange crew and fly him to the Vineyard and then to Lenox.

Shep was still at his desk.

"Do you have any plans or photographs of either Rod's house or the plant, or both?"

"I'll see what I can find."

"The project is growing. We'll have a security briefing from Doug later. And Doug is arranging our ground transport. And find those keys Rod says he has to the plant. All of them."

"Anything else?"

"Do you possess a false moustache and a wig?" Stone asked.

"What for?"

"Doug has pointed out that you're well known in Lenox, and you're the guy we're supposed to be hiding."

"No, I have neither of those things. I've got sunglasses and a tweed cap. That's the best I can do."

Stone sighed. "Oh, well."

Shep went back to his tasks, and Stone sat down to make some notes of his own, embarrassed by Doug's assessment of his plan.

THIRTY-SIX

O n Saturday morning Fred drove out to Brooklyn, picked up Solomon Fink, drove him to Teterboro to the Strategic Services hangar, and installed him in the G-500. Sol was joined shortly by a six-man team from that agency, carrying considerable luggage.

They took off, made the short flight to Martha's Vineyard, and set down.

S tone gathered his group, including the two women, and boarded the aircraft. Sol rose to greet him. "How was your flight, Sol?" Stone asked.

"Just marvelous. We're leaving again?"

"Yes, we have to fly to Lenox, Massachusetts, in the Berkshire Hills, and land for the night. We'll be staying at the Troutman house and having dinner there." He introduced Sol to the others, then they buckled in and were shortly on their way to Lenox. On landing, the airplane disgorged them into two gray Mercedes vans, each emblazoned with the name of DuctoVac, Cleaners of Heating and A/C Ducts.

Half an hour later they drove down a long, tree-lined drive to a stone mansion that looked as if it had been dismantled in the south of England, then reassembled in Massachusetts.

Once there, Shep assigned everyone to rooms and they dispersed until dinnertime, and afterward they reassembled in the library, where Doug conducted a chalk talk on the approaches to and the layout of the Troutman Industries plant. "Our goal," he said, "is to put that gentleman"—he pointed at Sol—"in this room." He tapped on the floor plan with his pointer. "We will enter the factory here"—he pointed at a door—"take the elevator to the third floor, and enter the office. We will encounter locks here, here, and on the safe we seek, here."

Sol spoke up, "Locks are my métier," he said. "Locks of all sorts, but particularly on safes."

"All of us," Doug continued, "will be wearing coveralls with the company name, DuctoVac, emblazoned upon them, face masks—part of our story is using strong disinfectants in the cleaning of ducts—and weapons concealed underneath. No man is to draw a weapon unless he is convinced that he is about to be fired upon, and no shots intended to be lethal will be fired. Is that understood?"

There was an affirmative mutter from the group.

"When we leave this house, you will take with you everything you brought. When our mission has been completed, we will reboard the vans and be driven directly to Pittsfield Airport, where we will reboard our airplane and depart for: first, the Vineyard, where we will deposit one group, and then, to Teterboro, where the remainder of you will deplane and continue back to where you came from. Mr. Fink, Stone's car will await you for the trip back to Brooklyn. This will be properly conducted, a simple mission, if we don't fuck it up. Any questions?" He answered a couple, then dismissed the group. "Departure from the house will be at nine AM."

After dinner, Stone and Brooke went to their room, while the others went to theirs.

"This is a beautiful house," Brooke said, looking out a window. "I'd like to take a walk in the garden."

"You are not here," Stone said, "so you cannot take a walk in the garden."

She looked at him blankly. "Then where am I?"

"In bed with me," Stone said, "and you cannot be seen outside the house."

"So this is all a big secret?"

"It is."

"What is this document you're trying to retrieve?"

"I'll tell you that after we have retrieved it and made our escape."

"Who are we escaping from?"

"The bad guys."

"Oh, in that case . . ." She fell into bed with him.

T he following morning their bags were collected, and they went downstairs for breakfast. At eight-forty-five, the group assembled in the drive and boarded the vans. As Stone entered and found his seat, he heard somebody's cell phone ring. Not his.

In the front passenger seat, Doug put his phone to an ear and spoke for a couple of minutes, then hung up. He turned and looked at Stone. "Unforeseen circumstances," he said.

"What?"

"Our people on the Vineyard picked up a conversation

aboard *Nostrovia* between a man they think was Kronk and an-other man."

"What were they saying?"

"That they were boarding a helicopter to be taken to the Troutman Industries factory, in Lenox."

Stone was alarmed. "When will they leave?"

"About ten minutes ago." He turned to his driver. "Hit it," he said. "The most speed you can make without getting ar-rested." Then he turned to Stone and the others behind them. "This operation is going to be conducted at double speed. Ev-erybody got that? Not a moment wasted."

"How long will it take them to get here?" Stone asked.

"I don't know what chopper they're flying, but let's say they'll fly at somewhere between 140 and 150 knots, so about an hour, if we're lucky."

"Swell," Stone said.

"We couldn't have predicted that," Doug said. "Oh, the pat-ent and the safe were mentioned."

Ten minutes later, they pulled up to the entrance to the building that Doug had selected for entry. Shep Troutman ran to the door and started trying keys from a clump Rod had given him. It took another five or six minutes to find one that worked, then they were inside.

Two men stayed with the vans and began pulling yards of tubing from them, to make them look busy cleaning ducts, while the others followed Doug inside. They took the elevator to the third floor and got out, facing a large door.

"Uh-oh," Shep said, pointing at the door. "*That* is a new lock, and none of my keys will fit it."

"Excuse me," Sol said, sweeping Shep aside. He set down his tool kit, opened it, selected two lock picks, then went to work. "Very clever lock," he muttered as he worked away. Ten minutes passed before there was a loud *click*, and the door opened. Across the room, a beam of morning sunlight illuminated the Excelsior.

Sol walked over to it and ran his fingers around the edges of the door, then he stopped at one point. "Here," he said, looking at his fingers, which were sticky. "This is where the combination was, but the tape has been removed."

Shep got into one of his pockets under the jumpsuit and produced three slips of paper. "My dad wasn't sure he could remember the combination," he said. "Try one of these, Sol."

Sol accepted the papers and looked at them. "There are three combinations here," he said. "We get only two tries, then the safe locks itself, and if that happens, it will take me more than an hour to open it."

"I thought it was three attempts," Shep said.

"Two," Sol replied. As he stepped forward toward the safe, the beating of a helicopter's rotors could be heard approaching.

"They've got a faster chopper than I had planned on," Doug said. "Get it open, Sol. I'm going downstairs to deal with our visitors and buy some time. When you're done here, put on your masks before you go out to the vans, and keep them on until we're off the property." He ran out of the room.

THIRTY-SEVEN

S hep took Sol's elbow and helped him toward the safe. "Take your time, Sol," he said.

"I always do," Sol replied. He fanned out the three pieces of paper, each with a combination. "Pick one," he said to Shep.

"I should think you'd be better at that," Shep replied.

"It doesn't matter who picks it. Only one of these is correct, maybe none at all."

Shep reached over and, without looking at them, picked one and handed it to Sol.

Sol pinned the piece of paper to the safe with thumb and forefinger, and read off the combination as he dialed it in. Sol pumped the lever on the door. "That ain't the one," he said. "Pick another."

———————

Doug came out of the building with a coil of tubing over his shoulder. There were four men gathered with his two at the rear of a van. One of them Doug recognized as Gregor Kronk.

"Ah, here he is now," Doug's man said. "Sir, I've been explaining about our annual service and about the toxins involved."

"What's to explain? If you go in there before the toxicity has abated you'll get lung cancer pretty soon and die not long after that." He looked at his watch. "You've got another thirty-seven minutes before you can enter unharmed."

"Do you have any extra masks?" Kronk asked.

"Nope. Each man is custom-fitted with his own mask. It fits only him, and we don't have any spares. Excuse me, please." He turned and went back into the building.

Upstairs, Sol entered the second combination and worked the handle. "No good," he said.

"But isn't it irretrievably locked up now?"

"No, but the work will take a while."

Doug walked into the room. "I've bought you another half hour," he said. "After that, I guess we'll just have to shoot it out with them."

Sol removed a stethoscope from his bag, plugged it into his ears and pressed the other end against the safe while he spun the knob. Then he began slowly turning the knob, listening carefully. "Write these numbers down as I dictate them," he said to Shep, who grabbed a pen and pad from the desk.

"How did you hold those guys off?" Stone asked Doug.

"I told them that if they came in here without a mask they'd get lung cancer and die."

"That would do it," Stone said. "Was Kronk among them?"

"Yes, but I had my mask on, so he didn't recognize me."

S ix minutes," Shep said. Sol was still slowly turning the knob and, occasionally, speaking a number. Finally, he stopped, took a deep breath and sighed.

"No luck?" Shep asked.

Sol reached out, grasped the lever, and pulled it down. The door of the Excelsior opened. He glanced at his watch. "That's a new record for me," he said.

Shep stepped over to the safe, swung the door open, and peered inside; there was only one item in the safe. "Here we go," he said. He reached inside and removed a leather letter-sized envelope and opened it. "We've got about twenty sheets here." He removed them from the stack, riffled through them, then returned them to the pouch. "Let's get out of here." He tucked the envelope inside his jumpsuit, put on his mask and his tweed cap, and headed for the door.

Stone waited while Sol closed and locked the safe and put his tools away, then they walked to the elevator together. Sol seemed very tired.

"Are you feeling all right, Sol?" Stone asked.

"I seem to be a little more tired than usual. I haven't worked for a long time."

"You can have a nap on the airplane," Stone said, tucking him into the elevator with the others.

"Masks on, everybody," Doug said.

On the ground floor, they walked to the rear door, opened it, and started toward the vans.

"Is it safe now?" Kronk asked Doug.

Doug consulted his watch. "Yes, but one of our men got a whiff." He indicated Sol, who was being helped into the van. "I hope he'll be all right in a few minutes. I'd give it another fifteen minutes before you go in, just to be on the safe side," he said, then got into the van. "If you'll excuse us, we have another job in Boston, and we're running late." He turned to the driver. "Get us out of here, normal pace, no hurry."

Five minutes later they were on the road to the airport. Doug picked up his phone and pressed a button. "Start the right engine," he said. He looked into the back seat. "As soon as we stop, start peeling the logos off the sides of the vans. We'll dump the boiler suits at Teterboro."

The vans came to a halt, and everyone went into action. Stone assisted Sol out of the van, and with the help of the stewardess, got him aboard and buckled into his seat. "Would you like some coffee, Sol?"

"Sure," Sol replied, "as long as it has brandy in it."

Stone nodded to the stewardess and tucked a blanket around Sol. A moment later, the last person was aboard and the left engine was starting. As soon as it had spooled up they were taxiing, and five minutes after that, they had lifted off and were making their first turn.

A cheer went up from the passengers.

Doug was sitting across the aisle from Stone. "I can't believe we pulled that off," he said.

"You're surprised?" Stone asked. "I *expected* you to pull it off."

Sol brightened as he sipped his coffee. "I'm much better now."

"You'll drop us off at the Vineyard," Stone said, "then you'll continue on to Teterboro, have a ride in the Bentley, and you're home."

The Gulfstream set down at the Vineyard airport, discharged its passengers, and soon was headed for Teterboro.

———

Back at the Troutman house in the Vineyard, Stone watched as Shep sat down at the library table with his father, opened the leather envelope, and handed Rod the papers inside.

Rod flipped slowly through them.

"The multilathe is there," Shep said.

"And that's not all," Rod replied. "There are twenty-one other patents for various pieces of equipment. I had forgotten about most of them."

"Are they valuable?" Shep asked.

"Only to the extent that the business can't be run without them," Rod replied.

"Well, Shep," Stone said, "I think we're in a better bargaining position with Kronk if those are tucked into your safe."

Doug spoke up, "No, you're not."

Stone sat up. "And why not?"

"Men like Kronk don't bargain," Doug said. "They take what they want and eliminate anybody who gets in their way."

THIRTY-EIGHT

Kronk and his people stood around, checking their watches every two or three minutes. "I've got a feeling we've been had," Kronk said. He walked over to the door, opened it, and sniffed the air. "You smell anything?" he asked Mueller.

"No, sir."

"That's because there isn't anything to smell. There never was."

"Then let's get our guy up there and get that safe opened." Mueller led the way up to his office, unlocked it, and walked in. There was a slip of paper on his desk. "What's this?" he asked the safe man.

"It's the combination to the safe," the man replied, taking the paper, walking to the safe, and dialing in the combination.

He operated the handle, and the door swung open. "There you are," he said. "Anything else?"

Kronk switched on a desk lamp, illuminating the interior of the safe. "Empty," he said. "Whatever there was is gone. Certainly the patent."

"How do you know there is a patent?" Mueller asked.

Kronk took a sheet of paper from his inside pocket and handed it to him.

Mueller read it out loud. "'Dear Sirs: We wish to enter negotiations for the renewal of our license on the patents for the multilathe and several other pieces of equipment.'" He looked at Kronk. "Several other patents? What are those for?"

"Maybe our customers can tell us," Kronk said. "Or Mr. Shepherd Troutman."

S tone woke up the following morning, and he felt more tired than usual. Maybe that was because Brooke had felt energized by their excursion and had, the night before, made it plain. "We need to leave today," he said to her. "Better get packed." He made the necessary calls to Joan.

They had breakfast in bed, then went down to where everybody else sat around the kitchen table. "Brooke and Dino and I are headed back to New York this morning," Stone said.

"You need a lift?" Doug asked.

"No, we've got the scooters," Stone said. "About the patents, Shep: I think I should take them back to my office."

"I suppose they would be more secure there," Shep admitted.

"It's not just that. I need to have patent attorneys read them, renew them where necessary, and assess their value. After that, well, I've got an Excelsior myself. They'll be there when you need them."

The M2 was waiting for them when they arrived at the FBO. They checked in the scooters, set their bags out for the pilot to stow, then boarded and buckled up.

"You think that's the end of all this?" Dino asked.

"No," Stone replied.

Stone, having dropped off Brooke, went home, changed into a suit, and went down to his office. He made a call to the head of the patents department at Woodman & Weld. "Can you send an armed guard over here for what I've got?" Stone asked.

"Sure. Are you expecting trouble?"

"Yes, I am. When you get this package you should photocopy the patents, then return the originals. Let me know what you think of them as soon as you've had a chance to read them."

"Certainly."

Stone hung up and handed the leather envelope to Joan.

"Make us a copy of these, then the originals will be picked up by an armed messenger, copied there, and returned to us."

Joan trotted off to do her work.

S tone was working his way through his phone messages when Joan came into his office. "There's a man named Kronk— Is that a real name?"

"Yes, it is. What about him?"

"He's here to see you. He doesn't have an appointment."

"Where are the copies you made of the patents?"

"In the Excelsior."

"And the leather envelope?"

"That went with the originals to Woodman & Weld."

"Good. You can show Mr. Kronk in, and don't put any calls through while he's here."

Kronk entered looking dry-cleaned and well-pressed. "Good day, Mr. Barrington."

"Good day, Mr. Kronk. I'm surprised to see you. Has your cruise ended?"

"It has."

"I hope you enjoyed yourselves."

"Moderately well," Kronk replied.

"What can I do for you?"

"Where is Mr. Shepherd Troutman?"

"I'm afraid I still don't know. I haven't heard from him."

"I would like you to contact him."

"I'm afraid I have no means to do that."

"His cell phone will do."

"Mr. Troutman turned off his cell phone, on my advice, after he was assaulted, for the second time, in Central Park. I don't believe he has turned it back on since that time."

"You said you knew where to send your clients' bills. Where do you send Mr. Troutman's?"

"To a post office box in Lenox, Massachusetts."

"I believe we nearly met there, this morning," Kronk said.

"You and Mr. Troutman?"

"And you, as well."

"I've been here all morning, since my return from the Vineyard."

"By what means did you return?"

"Via a light jet, belonging to a business associate."

"Did Mr. Troutman return with you?"

"Mr. Kronk, I've already told you, I am unaware of the whereabouts of Mr. Troutman. Our airplane was a small one; I'm sure if he had been aboard I would have noticed."

"I dislike being lied to," Kronk said.

"I dislike being called a liar," Stone replied.

"Mr. Troutman is in possession of documents that should have been conveyed to me upon the sale of Troutman Industries."

"I've read that sales contract," Stone said, "and there was

no reference therein to any documents being part of that transaction."

"Nonsense."

"I'll ask my secretary to bring me the contract. Perhaps you can point out the reference to me." Stone reached for his phone.

Kronk held up a staying hand. "Don't bother. The inclusion of the documents in the sale was implied."

"Neither do I recall any such implication, though such would hardly have been sufficient to transfer ownership of anything."

"I am so advised by counsel."

"Then perhaps you should obtain new counsel, one who didn't fail the contracts class in law school."

"Please deliver a message from me to Mr. Troutman," Kronk said.

"I'd be happy to, if he should be in touch, which I doubt."

"Tell him that, if I do not receive the documents posthaste, he is going to need new counsel, and a new head."

"I note the threat in your request, Mr. Kronk."

"I'm so glad to hear it." Kronk got up and walked out.

THIRTY-NINE

Stone called Mike Freeman.

"Good morning, and welcome back."

"I had a visit from Gregor Kronk this morning."

"I thought he was still in Massachusetts."

"So did I."

"What did he want?"

"Two things: the patents and Shep Troutman's head," Stone said. "We've got to review and reconstruct Shep's security, and we've got to get him out of the Vineyard and keep him out of Massachusetts."

"How soon?" Mike asked.

"Before Kronk figures out how many times I've lied to him."

"You could fly the lot of them to your house in England."

"I think if you googled me, that house would turn up, first thing. I've hidden there too often."

"Key West?"

"Too hot, and the house is too small to hold everybody in comfort."

"The Paris house?"

"Too small."

"Your house in L.A. is infinitely expandable." Mike spoke of the house Stone had built for his late wife, Arrington, when he had sold her property there to build the Arrington Hotel. She had not survived to see it.

"That's a good point," Stone said. A green light flashed on his phone. "Hold on, please." He picked it up. "Yes?"

"The queen is on line one."

Stone told Mike he'd get back to him later, then pressed the button. "Yes?"

"This is the White House operator. Will you accept a call from the president of the United States?"

"Of course."

A click. "Hello there. Where are you these days?"

"In New York. I just got in from a few days on Martha's Vineyard."

"That sounds pleasant."

"Believe me, it was mostly work."

"Where are you for the next few days?"

"I'll be in L.A. tomorrow. How about you?"

"I think it would be nice if I were in L.A., too," she said. "I have a speech to make there, but I can tack on a couple of days without getting impeached, I think."

"Then I will look forward to seeing you."

"You will be alone, then?"

"I'll have two male guests, clients."

"Then we'll meet at the guest cottage between the houses."

"Perfect. Dinner tomorrow night, in the cottage?"

"Perfect, indeed. Looking forward." She hung up.

Stone buzzed for Joan. "I'm off to L.A. in the morning. Let Faith know, so she can assemble a crew. We'll need the G-500, wheels up at nine AM. First stop, Martha's Vineyard, next stop Burbank."

"Done," she said.

"Also, I'm going to need ten double rooms in the hotel for security people."

"Your wish, etcetera, etcetera." She hung up.

Stone called Mike Freeman back. "Okay, L.A. is on. I've booked ten double rooms for your people. Shep and Rod can stay at my house. We'll pick them up at the Vineyard airport at ten AM tomorrow. Let Doug know."

"We're going to need another airplane for my people and their equipment. I'll get our L.A. office started on setting up communications today."

"Okay, give me a few minutes to break the news to Shep." They both hung up.

Stone messaged Shep: Call me back on a secure line.

A couple of minutes later, Shep was on the phone.

"How's it going?" he asked.

"Not great. Have you had any problems there?"

"Not yet, but everybody is pretty tense."

"Neither you nor Rod is safe at that location any longer, so we're moving you both tomorrow. You can shut down that house. Doug will have you at the airport at ten AM, where my Gulfstream will pick you up. I'll be aboard."

"This is a royal pain in the ass," Shep said. "Where are we going?"

"I'm not going to tell you. You'll know when you arrive. Don't worry, the surroundings will be more pleasant there than they have been at your present location."

"I'm not sure Dad is going to buy this."

"Tell him the alternative is to be sedated and crated for shipment, and not to speak a word of this to the staff there or anyone else."

"Oh, all right."

"And keep your cell phones turned off. We don't want you tracked."

"I understand, but Dad won't. He hates flying."

"Tell him, if you must, that he will be aboard the most comfortable airplane on earth."

"Is that true?"

"Almost." Stone hung up.

D ino called. "Dinner tonight?"

"Sure."

"P.J.'s at seven?"

"Done. I'm off again tomorrow. We have to relocate Shep and Rod."

"Where?"

"Tell you later." Stone hung up.

They were halfway to P. J. Clarke's when Fred said, "Excuse me, sir. We're being followed."

"By what?"

"A van. Maybe another vehicle, as well."

"Shit," Stone said.

Dino was already at the table when he arrived. "Tell your people I was followed here."

"You want your tail rousted?"

"That would be very satisfying. There's a van and maybe one other vehicle."

Dino spoke a few lines into his phone, then hung up. "They're about to get a lesson in NYPD etiquette."

A drink was brought for Stone, and menus.

"So, now can you tell me where you're off to?"

Stone drew invisible letters on the tablecloth.

"Gotcha."

"Want to go along?"

"Can't do it. I'm getting ragged about my Vineyard tan, this time by the mayor. I need to be seen at my desk, even if others are doing the work."

"I can appreciate your need to be seen hard at work," Stone said.

One of Dino's men came to the table. "We have a van and an SUV and four men in custody. What do you want them charged with?"

"I'm sure they've violated some traffic ordinance or other," Dino said. "Just see that they're housed overnight. No phone calls."

"If you can hold them until, say, noon tomorrow," Stone said, "that would be very helpful."

"The NYPD is all about helpful," Dino said.

FORTY

Dino called Stone early. "I'll have my detail pick you up at eight AM," he said. "The Bentley attracts too much attention."

"Three police cops with flashing lights and whoopers don't attract attention?"

"They'll think it's me," Dino said. "We've had a dozen calls overnight from Kronk or his lawyers. He's steamed; you oughta know that."

"I'll write it down," Stone said. He went back to his packing, which was light; he had clothes in L.A.

They pulled into the Strategic Services hangar at eight-thirty, and they had used the whoopers only twice. Stone took

Faith, his pilot, aside. "I want the satphones shut down now. No outgoing calls, unless I say so. Also, have the stewardess collect everybody's cell phones, including mine." He boarded and buckled in.

They set down in the Vineyard shortly before ten, and taxied to a little-used area of the ramp, where a large van unloaded the crowd from the Troutmans' Vineyard house. They were rolling down the runway at ten o'clock.

"Now can you tell us where we're going?" Shep asked.

"Not until she's done," Stone said, pointing to the stewardess, who was collecting phones in a basket and labeling them. Stone gave her his phone. "Yours and Rod's, too," he said to Shep, who grumbled, but gave them up. "Can I use the satphone?"

"It's out of service," Stone replied.

"For how long?"

"Until I say so."

"We appear to be headed west."

"Good guess, Shep."

"How far west?"

"We refueled on the Vineyard, so we have the range for Hawaii."

"Jesus!"

"Also, Vancouver, San Francisco, L.A., San Diego, or Puerto Vallarta. Take your pick."

"A tracker could look us up on the FlightAware website."

"We don't appear there. Also, the pilot filed for St. Louis but will change our destination with ATC en route."

"How will I pass the time?" Shep asked.

"Books, magazines, a movie, or my favorite, sleep. Rod has already taken that suggestion." He nodded at the sleeping elder Troutman across the aisle, with a cashmere blanket tucked up to his chin and his seat reclined.

"If he's out like that," Shep said, "this must truly be the most comfortable airplane on the planet." In ten minutes, he was asleep. He didn't wake up until the landing gear came down.

"Where are we?"

"Welcome to Honolulu," Stone said. "You'll get your phone back when we reach our lodgings." Hawaiian music played softly over the sound system. They got into a Mercedes van and were driven directly to Stone's house on the Arrington Hotel property.

"I'm confused," Shep said, looking around.

"Good. Imagine how Mr. Kronk must feel. You and your dad are in the downstairs bedrooms next to the library. Our luggage will be along shortly in another van."

"May I have my phone back now, please?" Shep asked.

"No. It's important that no one in our party makes a cell call until certain electronic details are taken care of that will make all our calls appear to be originating in New York. Give it an hour. After that, log every call you make by number and minutes."

"Okay, I'm impressed," Shep said.

"You should be: it's costing you a hell of a lot of money. Just staying alive can be expensive at times."

Stone picked up a house phone in his study. "May I speak to the head of the Secret Service detail, please?"

"Of course, Mr. Barrington."

"Jack Dunn," a voice said.

"Agent Dunn, this is Stone Barrington."

"How are you, Mr. Barrington? I'm afraid it will be another two hours before she's in the residence. She instructed me to tell you that dinner will be at seven o'clock, in the cottage between the two houses." The two houses were Stone's and the Presidential Mansion, kept by the hotel for visiting heads of state or tycoons who were willing to pay outrageously for lodging.

"Thank you, Jack. I'll see her then." He hung up and found Shep Troutman at his elbow.

"Dad is continuing his nap," he said. "Where's this cottage where you're having dinner?"

"Next door. A friend of mine is staying at the large house beyond that, and we're meeting halfway. You and your father will be dining here, at six-thirty."

"I guess that's satisfactory."

"I hope so, because you're not getting off the ranch while we're here. You'd probably run into someone you know in the hotel dining room. Or someone you don't want to know."

"I get the picture," Shep said.

"By the way, I'm keeping your cell phone, but you can make outgoing calls on the house phones. Not a word about where you are, though, or all this money will have been wasted."

"I take your point."

"Why didn't you bring Phil with you?"

"I asked her, but she declined. She has a commission to finish and a business to run, she said."

"She probably didn't take to being shot at, either."

"You could say that."

"Few people do, and you want to avoid them."

"Good advice."

"Good advice is my work," Stone said. "Not taking it can be dangerous."

"Stone, I don't need impressing any further, please."

"I'm glad to hear it. Why don't you go and have a chat with the butler about what you'd like for dinner and what wines you'd prefer? You may order anything to eat but foie gras."

"Why not foie gras?"

"It has to come from out of state. We'd have to find a bootlegger."

"Who's your friend next door?" Shep asked.

"That's a state secret," Stone replied.

"That gives me a hint."

"Try and appreciate it, because it's all you're going to get out of me."

"Aha!"

"Careful. If you get too curious, somebody will have to shoot you in the head."

"My curiosity is quelled," Shep said, then went upstairs.

FORTY-ONE

Stone had not entered the cottage for a long time. He had forgotten how charming it was. A merry fire burned in the living room fireplace, which was nice for the chilly California nights, and a huge sofa faced the hearth.

She sneaked up behind him. "Hello, stranger," she said.

Stone jumped, then turned to receive both her and the drink in her hand. She kissed him on the ear with a flick of her tongue. "You always remember what I like," he said, sipping the bourbon.

"It helps that we both drink the same booze," she said. "And that we both have tongues."

"Good point."

"I locked the door behind you, so we can't be disturbed,

except by the butler, who has been ordered not to emerge until I ring for him."

They fell onto the big sofa, and she arranged her legs across his lap. He had not realized until then that she was wearing nothing under a silken garment, and that could be seen through, just a bit.

"I can see your nipples," he said.

"Oh, good. That will make them easier to find when you start looking. Let's finish our drinks, first, though. I like a little buzz with my sex."

"How do you manage when I'm not around?" he asked.

"I have a secretary who likes to browse in sex shops. Now and then she smuggles in a toy for me."

"Sounds like you hardly need me."

"If you'd like to be useful, you can switch it on later."

"I hope I can be more useful than that."

"I'm sure you will be," she said, "based on past experience."

They finished their drinks and toyed with each other until hunger overtook them.

"Are you ready to dine?"

"Whenever you are."

"I bought you a gift," she said, reaching behind her and retrieving a large box, tied with a bow.

He opened it and found a dark blue silk dressing gown with white polka dots. "Oh, very nice," he said.

"One can shop at Turnbull & Asser online these days."

He stood up and tossed his loose clothing on a chair, then slipped into the robe. "Feels wonderful on the skin."

Holly picked up a little silver bell and gave it a ring. "Dinner now," she said, standing up and leading him to the table, pausing along the way to slip on another garment to conceal her semi-nakedness.

They sat down and the butler brought their first courses, each under a little dome. He snatched the covers away.

"Foie gras!" he exclaimed. "Wherever did you find it?"

"I brought it from the White House," she said. "I knew you would be feeling deprived."

"I certainly was." He tasted a bite. "Just perfect."

They were served a roast duck as a main course, and the butler carved for them. Finally, he brought a slice of pineapple upside-down cake, with a scoop of rum raisin ice cream on top, a favorite of his.

They moved back to the sofa and dawdled over cognac.

"Whatever have you been up to?" Holly asked.

"I'm hiding a client and his father from some evil Russians."

"Which evil Russians?"

"Fellow named Kronk."

Her eyebrows went up. "That name crossed my desk—or rather, the Situation Room table—earlier this week. My people wanted to throw him out of the country, but unfortunately, he is a naturalized American citizen."

"I think you can take it for granted that, if that is so, his application for citizenship was somehow fraudulent."

"Why do you say that?"

"Because everything about him is somehow fraudulent. Right now, I'm in the not-so-enviable position of possessing something he will, very shortly, desperately need." He explained about the patents.

"And what are you going to do about that?"

"I'm going to try to think of a way to use them to get him off my client's back."

"And out of the country for good?"

"That is devoutly to be wished, but more than I could ever come up with."

"Let me see what I can do to help," she said.

"If you can, do it without ever mentioning my name," Stone said.

"Not speaking your name is not a problem. Dealing with Kronk may be."

"I don't doubt it."

"Have you spoken to Lance Cabot about him?" she asked.

"Not yet. I was saving that for when I had an actual idea about what might be done about Kronk."

"Then don't. Let's try and go around Lance this time."

"That will be fine, as long as he never finds out. If he does, he'll never let me forget it."

"You forget that before I was in the White House, I was Lance's assistant. Nobody knows him better."

"That's good, because Lance always seems to be one jump ahead of me."

"That is Lance's specialty," Holly said. "Maybe we can go through Lance, if whatever I learn can be proposed to him as your idea, which he can take credit for."

Stone laughed. "I like the sound of that. I hope Lance has not replaced one of my buttons with a microphone," he said.

"You are not wearing any buttons," she said, loosening his garment. "So speak freely." She kissed him in a very nice place.

"I'm speechless," Stone breathed.

I t was deep into the wee hours before Stone picked up Holly and carried her to her bed, still sleeping like a child. He pulled back the covers and tucked her in, then he tiptoed out of the cottage and made his way back inside his house.

"Good morning," a deep voice said, making him jump.

Stone looked into the library and saw Rod Troutman sitting before a fire, reading a book.

"I couldn't sleep," Rod said.

"I sometimes have that problem," Stone said. "Would you like a pill?"

"I think not. I'll finally switch off, then I can sleep late."

"Don't forget to put out the 'Do Not Disturb' sign," Stone said.

"I'll remember," Rod said. "How are things on the national front?" he asked. "Any wars looming?"

"I have no idea what you're talking about," Stone said, then went upstairs to bed.

"Nice dressing gown," Rod called from downstairs.

FORTY-TWO

Stone's cell phone rang at 6:00 AM, and he struggled to answer.

"Hello?" he finally managed, hoarsely.

"It's Lance. Where are you?"

"Three time zones west of you," Stone said.

"I'll call you back, but you may be dead by then."

"Wait a minute!"

"Yes?"

"What do you mean, I may be dead by then?"

"Among the unloving, an ex–Stone Barrington."

"I'm awake now. Please explain yourself."

"A source has picked up a rumor that you are scheduled for permanent demolition."

"Lance, I didn't get to bed until two AM and now it's six. Please explain, or the hell with it, I'll roll over and die."

"You've had dealings with a man named Kronk, I believe."

"You believe falsely. I have gone far out of my way to *not* have dealings with him."

"Same thing."

"Anyway, it's my client he wants to kill."

"Young Troutman?"

"Yes."

"I knew his father. He fell off the perch recently, did he not?"

"Not. He wished it to be seen that way, so he undertook to disappear. I'm helping."

"By withholding the patents?"

"Why do you need me? You already know everything."

"Perhaps so, but there are things you don't know."

"Enlighten me."

"Each of the patented machines has an internal clock and calendar. When the license for the patent runs out, the machine turns off and can only be restarted by activating a code in its software. The licensee pays for that code, which gives him access to the machine for another five or ten or whatever days, months, or years."

"I'm not sure my client is aware of that."

"He must be aware, or he could not have been operating his machinery for all these years."

"That's very interesting," Stone said. "I believe I'll have to bring it to his attention and ask why he's never told me that."

"What would you have done differently, if you had known?"

"Well, I would have . . ."

"Complete that sentence, please."

"I don't know what I would have done differently."

"Maybe that's why he hasn't bothered to tell you."

"That could be—annoyingly—true."

"How else may I be of service to you, Stone?"

"Let's start by telling me why you phoned me at five AM."

"It is six AM, but let's not quibble."

"Never mind, I'm going back to sleep. You may phone me after nine AM, California time." Stone hung up and fell back on the bed, falling asleep almost immediately.

The doorbell rang. Stone looked at the bedside clock. Seven AM. "What?"

"Your breakfast, sir. You ordered it for seven."

Stone groaned. "Come in!"

A waiter struggled in and placed a silver tray on his lap. "May I pour you some coffee, sir?"

"Thank you, no. I always have coffee after breakfast."

"As you wish sir." He placed copies of the *Los Angeles Times* and the *New York Times* on the bed and left.

It surprised Stone how hungry he became when he saw the scrambled eggs and sausages. He ate them greedily, washed down by orange juice, then poured himself some coffee and shook out the *New York Times.*

A headline in the lower left-hand corner of the front page caught his eye. *RASH OF HOUSE FIRES IN MARTHA'S VINE-YARD*, it read. Stone read quickly, then turned to the inside page to finish:

> *Three large beachfront houses burned to the ground last night along a stretch of highly desirable beachfront on this tony isle, each of them valued north of ten million dollars. Police and fire chiefs assume arson, but have no suspects.*

"Well, *I* have a suspect," Stone said aloud to himself.

"What?" someone said.

Stone turned and found Shep Troutman standing in the open doorway.

"Bad news," Stone said.

"I've already read the *Times* piece."

"I suspect that the time clock has run out on Kronk's machines," Stone said.

"How do you know about the time clocks?" Shep asked.

"Well, I sure didn't hear it from you," Stone said, hotly.

"What good would it have done if I had mentioned it?"

"We'll never know, will we? On the other hand, if you had mentioned that time was running out immediately, we might have beefed up security or otherwise anticipated his actions."

"You could have done that anyway."

"Protect empty houses that were not under threat? I'm not psychic, and I wasn't hired to protect empty houses. I think you'd better scare up some local security in Lenox for the family manse. That's all the advice I have to offer at the moment. Close the door on your way downstairs to explain this to your father. And by the way, you might pass the news on to your neighbors."

"My neighbors?"

"The owners of the other two houses that burned. You'd better call your insurance company, too. Those people may tend to blame you."

"I am the owner of the other two houses," Shep said. "And when I became very, very wealthy, I canceled all such insurance and self-insured."

"So, you rolled the dice and came up snake eyes, I believe the expression is?"

"I did, and I did," Shep said. "And now I'll rebuild them without a second thought for what they cost me." He turned and went downstairs.

Stone continued with the newspaper, and switched on CNN as well. The arson on the Vineyard was now getting national, perhaps worldwide attention. He switched it off.

Then, from downstairs, he heard a deep-throated shouting. "You canceled the goddamned insurance on the houses? Are you out of your fucking mind?"

"Self-insurance is a good way to save money, if you can afford it!" Shep yelled back. "I was just unlucky!"

"Self-insurance and unlucky is a bad combination!" Rod yelled.

Stone turned on the TV again.

FORTY-THREE

Stone was just out of the shower when the house phone rang. "Yes?"

"It's your next-door neighbor," she said. "How would you like to take a drive?"

"What, in a motorcade?"

"Suppose I could figure a way of doing it without an obvious motorcade?"

"How?"

"I seem to remember that you own a 1950s-era Mercedes-Benz 300S convertible."

"The bright red one? Yes. And you think that would be less conspicuous than a motorcade?"

"I've worked out a plan with the Secret Service: First, they will drive ordinary-looking vehicles. Second, they will be spread out several car lengths, instead of right on the bumper. Third, the occupants will be male-female couples, wearing casual clothes."

"Something, I hope, that will hide the machine guns and shotguns."

"Of course."

"And what is the purpose of this jaunt, besides inhaling extra carbon dioxide?"

"I'm thinking of buying a house in Malibu. A secret showing has been arranged."

"Then could we just dispense with the Secret Service detail entirely, and I'll carry something."

"No, part of the showing is to have the house inspected by those officers to see if it can be defended. And the people showing it are offering us lunch on the deck."

"Lunch sold me," Stone said. "What time?"

"An hour?"

"I can do that." They both hung up.

Stone dialed the hotel garage. "This is Stone Barrington," he said. "You have an elderly Mercedes convertible of mine under wraps down there. Would you kindly unwrap it, make sure it will start, then wash it and deliver it to the president's house?"

"Of course, Mr. Barrington. What time would you like it?"

"In fifty-five minutes, please."

"Certainly, sir."

Stone got himself together and, at the stroke of the hour, he spoke to the Troutmen. "I'm going out for a few hours," he said. "Your security team is aware."

"Can we go out?" Rod asked.

"Not unless you want to greatly increase your chances of dying today." He walked over to the house next door, where the four-door convertible was waiting, gleaming, top down. He got behind the wheel.

A moment later, Holly came out of the house, wearing dark glasses, a head scarf, and a baby blue surgical mask. The door was opened for her, and she got in and handed Stone a plaid face mask.

"I thought most people weren't wearing these anymore," he said.

"I am, for obvious reasons. And you are, because I am," she replied.

"That makes perfect sense," he said. "Sort of." He started the car, put it in gear, and drove off the property. The Secret Service, true to their word, kept their social distance.

"Where are we going?" Stone asked.

"I told you, Malibu. All you have to do is follow the green sedan up ahead."

The weather was what California always promised it would be, without the fires, earthquakes, or mudslides that so frequently intruded upon the peace of its inhabitants. They drove down Sunset Boulevard, all the way to the sea, and turned right on the Pacific Coast Highway. They followed the road some miles, through Malibu proper to the handsome development called Malibu Colony. The green lead car stopped briefly at the guarded gate, then the loose motorcade was allowed through.

"The garage door should be open," Holly said. "Drive in."

They followed the green car, until it slowed and the passenger pointed to an open garage. Stone drove in, and the door closed behind them.

"Here we are!" Holly said cheerfully, then got out and removed her mask and scarf. Stone did the same and followed her into the house.

They entered a bright hallway that led to a large living room, blindingly lit by sunlight.

"Wow," Holly breathed. "It's better than the brochure."

"Madame President," a woman in a business suit said, walking toward her with an outstretched hand. Holly didn't introduce Stone. They followed the woman on a tour lasting nearly an hour, while Holly inspected every nook, cranny, and cupboard in the house. The agent then led them down to the deck where a table was set for lunch, and said goodbye, leaving them alone with a couple from the Secret Service, who took chairs near the south railing.

"What do you think?" Holly asked.

"It's lovely. And expensive."

"The agent says they're asking twelve million but will take ten."

"Wow, what a bargain!" Stone said. "Can you afford it?"

"I can if I sign the book contract I've been offered, after my term is up."

"Can you afford the California income taxes? Ex-presidents have to pay those, too, you know."

"You're trying to take the fun out of this, aren't you?"

"No, I'm just trying to cast a little sunshine on the plan. Tell me how you view yourself five years from now."

"Try one year," she replied.

Stone was stunned. "Are you really thinking of not running for reelection?"

"I wouldn't be, if there weren't two or three highly suitable candidates lined up and waiting."

"Are you bored with the job?"

"'Bored' is too strong a word. I think it's good for the party if some of those well-qualified candidates share the experience. What's your opinion of all this?"

"Apart from a house in California, how would you like to also have houses in New York, London, Paris, and the English countryside, near the sea?"

"I can't afford that."

"You're missing the point," he said.

She got it. "Oh!"

"You hadn't considered marrying me?"

"You've never once mentioned marriage," she said. "Anyway, I'm not sure I'm cut out for it."

"How about living in sin? Without benefit of clergy, as they say."

"That sounds like a lot more fun."

"Holly, if you really, really want this house, I'll buy it for you today—as part of the bigger picture."

"Sin?"

"Sin."

"That's very tempting."

"That's what sin is for. Think about it."

"For how long?"

"For as long as you like."

They drove back to the Arrington, mostly silent.

"I've got to leave for Washington at six," she said.

"Think about me."

"That's all I *will* think about." She got out of the car and went inside.

"Well," Stone said to himself, "I've made her my best offer."

FORTY-FOUR

Stone had dinner with the Troutmen and Doug, the head of the security detail. "Have you given any thought to how you want to proceed?" Stone asked.

"I have," Shep said. "And I've come up with nothing."

"Whatever Shepherd concludes is all right with me," Rod said.

"It appears that what started all this is not just Kronk's greed, but the business of the patents. He believes that you deceived him by withholding them from inclusion in the sale."

"That's not true. I just didn't think of them."

"Now that you have, can you think of a way to use them to extricate yourself from this situation?"

"You mean, just give up the patents?"

"No, offer to sell them to him."

"For how much?"

"You've said they're worth as much as the business. Start at two hundred fifty million and let him bid you down a bit, so he'll feel that he's gotten a bargain."

"You mean, let him get the best of me?"

"You got the best of him in the original sale, didn't you? If he were a conventional businessman he would already have sued you to have the patents included, and he would have had a case, one that he might have won."

"But he's not a conventional businessman."

"He's not. He's a man who is accustomed to taking what he wants."

"How can I deal with somebody like that?"

"Let's try dealing with him as though he were an ordinary businessman, albeit a smart one. He might react well to the opportunity, instead of hunting you down and killing you, which wouldn't get him the patents anyway."

"Maybe it's worth a try," Shep said. "How will you approach him?"

"I'll invite him to another meeting at my office. How much will you take to give him the patents and walk away?"

"A hundred million."

"So I can accept an offer of that number or higher on your behalf?"

"I guess. Do I have to come to the meeting?"

"I think it would be better if you didn't. He's already angry with you. Angry with me, too, but less so. I think he regards me as just a lawyer."

"All right, set it up."

"I think it's best for me to meet him in New York. Are you content to stay here until we have a signed deal?"

"Yes, Dad and I are very comfortable here. May we use the pool?"

"The president is in residence next door, but she's leaving at six. Wait until after that. You don't want to butt heads with the Secret Service."

"You mean we've been living next door to the president?"

"You have."

"Do you know her?" Rod asked.

"We're old friends. I drove her out to Malibu for lunch today."

"I've often thought that would be a great place to have a house," Shep said.

Stone handed him the real estate agent's card. "She has a beauty for sale in the Colony. They're asking twelve million, but will take ten. The president looked at it today. But I don't think she'll buy it. I can find out, if you like it."

"All right, we'll drive out there."

"Let Doug set that up," Stone said. "Don't take any chances."

"I won't."

S tone was reading in his study later in the day when the house phone rang.

"Hello?"

"It's Holly."

"Hi, there. You still leaving?"

"Yes, I'm in the car now. I just wanted you to know that I've decided against buying the Malibu house. I've already told the agent."

"As you wish."

"As for living in sin, I can't agree to that until I've decided whether to run for reelection. And that decision could be some months away."

"I'll try and be patient."

"You? Never!"

"I said 'try.'"

"I'll be in touch," she said, and they both hung up.

Stone called Joan in New York.

"Hi, boss. Coming home anytime soon?"

"Tomorrow, I think. Listen. Did that guy, Kronk, leave a number with you?"

"Yes."

"Call him and see if you can make me a date with him in my office, the day after tomorrow. Tell him I may have a solution to our problem."

"Will do. Ten AM or two PM?"

"Ten. Let's get it over with." He hung up.

Five minutes later, Joan called back. "You're on with Kronk for ten AM the day after tomorrow."

"Good." As he hung up, he heard people come in the front door. Shep and Rod entered the study.

"What did you think of the house?"

"I loved it. I offered them nine million, furnished, and they accepted."

"When do you want to close?"

"As soon as possible."

"I'm going back to New York tomorrow morning, and I have a meeting with Kronk the following day. Let's wait until after that to set a closing. I'll get the Woodman & Weld office to have an attorney in the L.A. office to close for you."

"When will we be able to leave here?"

"Let's see how the meeting with Kronk goes, then we'll have a better idea."

"All right."

"The pool next door is available now, if you'd like a swim."

"Great idea."

"There are swimsuits in your chests of drawers in your rooms."

"Join us?"

"I'm in the middle of a good book," Stone said. "I'll stick with that."

They went to change, and Stone's phone rang. "Yes?"

"It's Joan. I just wanted to say that the gentleman, Kronk, sounded very happy about meeting with you. I was surprised, since he looks like such an unhappy man."

"Thanks for letting me know," Stone said. He hung up and wondered if Kronk being happy was good or bad for him.

FORTY-FIVE

Stone arrived back at Teterboro late the following afternoon, and Fred met him in the hangar and drove him
home. On the way in, Stone called Dino.

"Bacchetti."

"I'm nearly home. Do you still get hungry in the eve-
nings?"

"I do, and the wife is abroad. Patroon at seven?"

"You're on."

Over their first drink, Stone brought Dino up to date on the
Kronk situation.

"You think that will work?" Dino asked.

"I think he's probably as weary as we are by now. It just might work."

"The more I hear about Kronk, the more worried I get," Dino said.

"You hear about Kronk?"

"I didn't, until I started paying attention and asking questions. One thing I learned is that our Italian-American mob friends are scared shitless of him."

"What are their reasons?"

"They've had a couple of deals go wrong. Kronk reacted badly. They lost some people, and painfully."

"Just what I wanted to hear when I'm about to start dealing with him."

"Explain 'dealing.'"

"We're going to offer to sell him the patents."

"The only problem with that is," Dino pointed out, "that he believes he already owns them."

"Well, there is that."

"I believe that he could take an offer to sell them to him as an affront, so you'd better be very, very careful."

"Oh, I'll just be my usual, affable self."

"I'm not sure charm will be enough."

"We'll have to see."

"All right," Dino said. "Let's write ourselves a little scene. I'll start."

"Okay."

They pretended to negotiate for a moment, but got no-where. "You're being intractable," Stone said.

"That's right," Dino said, "I am. Do you think Kronk is go-ing to be more tractable?"

"You have a point," Stone said.

"I think you need to let him know, right off the bat, that you're not going to be a pushover."

"I'll think about that," Stone said, and they ordered dinner.

The following morning, promptly at ten, Joan showed Kronk into Stone's office. He didn't even look at Stone. "All right, Barrington, you asked for this meeting, what's on your mind?"

"I thought we might try and reach an accommodation that would be beneficial to both you and my client."

"I'll tell you what will be beneficial: give me the patents and a release."

"And what would you give us?"

"Your balls, to keep."

"That's not an accommodation, that's a threat."

"I'm glad you recognize it for what it is."

"If you persist in this manner, I'll tell you what we'll give you, if there's no accommodation."

"You? Give me?"

"My client will sit down at any computer in the world, enter a series of codes, and shut down every factory you are operating. The coded machinery will become nothing more than a rusting pile of scrap metal, and that will be its only value. Now, from that position, calculate the loss of your investment and of all the income you would have derived from it, if you had been more tractable."

"Tractable? What does this mean?"

"Cooperative. Nicer, even."

Kronk glowered at him. Then Stone thought his shoulders slumped just a bit. "What number would your client deem 'tractable'?"

"My client feels that the value of the patents and the software is equal to that of the factories."

"You're saying he wants another two hundred fifty million dollars?"

"I think I might be able to persuade him to be tractable."

"I'll offer him another hundred fifty million," Kronk said.

Stone shrugged. "I can't promise an outcome, but I'll put your offer to him today."

"I know you have his authority to make a deal. I want your answer now."

Stone buzzed Joan. "Print a copy of the patent transfer, and insert the figure of one hundred fifty million dollars."

"I won't be a moment," Joan said.

Stone and Kronk sat and stared at each other for three or four minutes.

Suddenly, Kronk spoke, "What do you think of an Italian restaurant called Mama Leoni's?" he asked. "It has been recommended to me."

"I think it closed many years ago," Stone said. "Instead, try Caravaggio, on East Seventy-Fourth Street."

"Like the painter?"

"Exactly."

"Is it very good?"

"Yes, and it has the charm of being open."

Joan bustled in with the contract and handed them each a copy.

"You may wish to consult your attorney," Stone said.

"I *am* an attorney," Kronk said. "In my spare time." He signed the contracts and handed them to Stone. Stone signed both copies and handed him back one.

"Now," Stone said. "Let's close this meeting as we began it, with a threat: if any move is made against my client, his properties, or me and mine, he retains the ability to shut you down."

"And he expects me to trust him?"

"He trusted you not to burn down his properties. Would you like to make an offer for the land?"

"I would not," Kronk said. "I will be happy with these." He held up the contract. "And the patents, if you please."

Stone buzzed Joan. "Bring me the patents, please."

Joan entered Stone's office, crossed it, went into the back room and returned shortly with the leather envelope. "There you are, sir."

Stone handed the envelope. "There you are, sir. These are the originals. We retain copies."

Kronk made to rise.

"Just a minute," Stone said.

Kronk stopped. "What is it?"

"There is the matter of payment."

"Ah, yes." He removed an envelope from an inside pocket, opened it, removed three pieces of paper, handed one to Stone, and returned the others to his pocket.

Stone looked at the paper; it was a cashier's check for $150 million. "What are the amounts of the other two checks?" he asked.

Kronk, for the first time ever, smiled. "You will never know," he said.

"Remember," Stone replied. "If my client is . . . interfered with, he can always shut you down."

"At his peril," Kronk said. He got up and left.

Stone took a deep breath, then buzzed Joan.

"Yes, sir?"

"Come in."

She entered, and he handed her the check. "Call our bank and have them confirm that this won't bounce when presented."

Joan left, then returned. "Good as gold," she said.

Stone picked up the phone and dialed a number.

"Hello?"

"You're one hundred fifty million dollars richer than you

were ten minutes ago," Stone said. "That should more than cover the houses."

"Yes. Are we free to move about now?"

"Where do you want to go?"

"We'll talk it over and let you know."

"I would suggest that you not go directly back to anywhere Kronk knows about, at least for a week or so."

"You said you have a property in England?"

"I did, and you are welcome to it. My airplane will be at your disposal when you need it."

"Thank you. I'll call." They both hung up.

FORTY-SIX

The next morning, Stone was arranging an assignation with Brooke Alley when Joan buzzed. "It's Shepherd Troutman, on line two."

"Seven at P. J. Clarke's?" he asked Brooke.

"Peachy," she replied. "Bye." She hung up.

Stone pressed the other button. "Shep?"

"Hi. We've figured things out," he said. "We'd like to fly back to New York the day after tomorrow, where I have to pick up some clothes from the apartment. Then, the day after that, may we stop at the Vineyard for a couple of hours, before continuing to England? I have to look at house plans with the architect; we're rebuilding all three houses, and we want to start immediately, so that if we spend some time in England, when we return to the Vineyard they'll have been framed."

"No, if you did that you'd have to clear out through customs and immigration at an international airport, like Boston Logan, before departing for England. Let me suggest an alternative."

"Shoot."

"Fly to Teterboro, as you planned, run your errands, then the following day, I'll have you flown to the Vineyard in a light jet, where you can have your meeting, then return to Teterboro for your international departure. I need some flight time for my logbook, so I'll fly you to the island and back myself. After that, you might wait another day before you depart for England, so you won't arrive late at night."

"All right, at which airport will we land?"

"At a private field on my property. You'll be met there and taken to the house."

"Fine."

"One other thing. I'm nervous about your being on the Vineyard, for even a short time. Can your architect meet you at the airport and show you the plans there?"

"Yes, there's a meeting room at the FBO. I'll book it."

"Very good. When you land at Windward Hall, which is my house, the property manager, Major Bugg, will meet and orientate you. There are cars on the property you can use, but I'd stay close to home for a week, before venturing to London. Give things enough time to cool down."

"Of course."

"My pilot, Faith, will call you about your departure time

from Burbank, and she will conduct the subsequent flight to England. By the way, the check for your deal with Kronk has been deposited and was declared good as gold by the bank."

"Then maybe I can afford to have a suit made in London."

"Good idea." They hung up. He called Faith and gave her the drill for Burbank and England, then he freshened up and left for Clarke's and the company of Brooke.

After dinner they returned to Stone's house and ran for the bedroom. Later, he told her of the travel plans he had made.

"Can I fly up to the Vineyard with you?" she asked. "I'd like to check in with Phil."

"I'm just going to fly Shep up there, where he'll meet with his architect and then return to Teterboro with me. There won't be any time for visits, and I want to get Shep off the island as soon as possible."

"But you made a deal with this man, Kronk, didn't you? We'll all be safe on the Vineyard."

"Yes, but I don't want to trust Kronk to keep the deal. He has a low boiling point, and he was still simmering when we met earlier today."

"Oh, all right," she said. Then she started his engine again.

The following day Stone called Mike Freeman, told him of the successful deal with Kronk, and made new security arrangements for Shep's travel, in both the U.S. and the U.K.

"You're taking the M2 to the Vineyard?" Mike asked.

"Yes, I'll fly myself. I need the hours to keep sharp."

"I think you ought to have a couple of my people on that flight," he said.

"How about one? It's a small airplane, compared to the G-500."

"Okay, as you wish."

Stone hung up.

Two days passed without further action or noise from Kronk, and Stone began to feel better about the deal he had made. That morning Fred drove Stone out to Teterboro, where he did a preflight inspection of the Citation M2 with the regular pilot.

"Would you like me to fly left seat?" the man asked.

"No, it's a single-pilot airplane, and I used to own it, so I have a lot of time in type. It's just a couple of hours over and back, with a little waiting time in between, and I need the time."

"Okay, enjoy it. It's a great little airplane." He walked away, then came back a minute later with four life jackets. "I know you wouldn't ordinarily wear these for a short over-water flight, but there's an FAA examiner in the hangar right now doing ramp inspections, so let's let him see you with these on, and you won't have to dig out the ones under the seats."

Shep and Rod arrived, along with their security man. Stone handed out the life jackets and explained why and how to use them, and they all got them on.

An hour later, Stone set down on Martha's Vineyard, and they all walked into the FBO, where Shep's architect greeted them. Stone found a flight magazine and made himself comfortable in the pilot's lounge. He did not order fuel for the flight back, as they had left Teterboro with full tanks, and there was ample fuel for the flight.

An hour and a half later the meeting broke up, and the Troutmen stood in the doorway talking, while Stone went out and did a quick walk-around of the airplane. After that, they put on their life jackets again and boarded; the security man making sure they were buckled in and knew how to inflate their life jackets. Stone started the engines and ran through the cockpit checklist. That done, he requested his IFR clearance from the tower and was given a clearance good for ten minutes.

He taxied to the end of the runway and ran through the pre-takeoff checklist. The tower cleared him for takeoff, and he taxied onto the runway. Then, without stopping, he advanced the throttles full forward and began to roll. He lifted off and reached out his right hand to raise the landing gear.

With that thought in his head, something went terribly wrong. There was a loud noise, and the windshield was gone, and moist air was blowing into the cockpit. Instinctively, Stone operated the landing gear to slow them down, but that didn't happen. He reached down and yanked his seat belt as tight as he could, while yelling, "Brace for impact!" at the top of his lungs.

The nose of the airplane was rising, and he shoved on the yoke to level it but got no response. Then, in seconds, the aircraft entered an aerodynamic stall, which meant it wasn't flying anymore, just falling, nose down. He placed a hand on the pull tab of the life jacket and yanked, filling in instantly with the CO_2 from the little bottle.

The airplane went into the water and he had the breath knocked out of him as he slammed against his five-point seat harness.

He came awake, floating in his seat and choking on seawater, then he managed to turn the knob on his chest that released his seat harness. The seat fell away from him and he bobbed to the surface, as the full jacket turned him onto his back, with his head supported.

After that he knew nothing until he felt himself being hauled into a rubber dingy. He lasted a minute or so, then passed out again.

FORTY-SEVEN

Stone woke in an examining room in a hospital, IVs in both arms, an oxygen mask strapped on, sitting up on a hard, barely cushioned table.

"He's awake," a young male voice said.

"Mr. Barrington?" a female voice said, and a bright light streamed into his eyes.

"Turn that off," Stone said.

The light went off. "It speaks," the woman said. "I am Dr. May Harris. You are at the Martha's Vineyard Hospital in Oak Bluffs, in the emergency room. Do you understand that?"

"I think so," Stone replied. "But why am I here?"

"You were flying an airplane that decided not to fly anymore."

"Did everyone survive?"

"No, only you and a man named Karl Walters. The two other passengers are deceased."

Stone winced. "What made the airplane stop flying?"

"There's a man here from the National Transportation Safety Board who can explain that better than I."

"How long have I been here?"

"About five hours."

"How did the NTSB get here so fast?"

"I believe they choppered your man to our pad from Logan. I'll get him for you."

"Wait," Stone said. "How badly am I hurt? I'm afraid to move."

"How do you feel?" she asked.

"I hurt all over," he said.

"We've already done the necessary scans. Miraculously, you have no broken bones and your internal organs are about where they're supposed to be. I'll give you something for the pain." She injected something from a syringe into his IV tube, and a moment later he felt a little rush of warmth.

"Better," he said.

"Be right back."

Stone luxuriated in the new lack of pain. Morphine, he guessed. What else could work so fast?

Dr. Harris returned with a man who, Stone thought, looked like ex-military: short, cropped hair, not much belly. "I'm Ray Leonard, NTSB," he said. "How you doing?"

"I'm drugged, thanks, so I'm okay. What happened?"

"There's going to be a long and very thorough investigation to determine that and to learn if this was a criminal event."

"Can you give me the short version?"

"Okay, but I'll deny telling you, if anybody asks."

"Your secrets are safe with me," Stone said.

"Right. Somebody stuck a bomb, probably a plastic explosive, into the aft portion of your airplane. When it exploded, the tail disappeared, and you took a dive into the drink. One of the passengers, a Karl Walters, got himself out and fired his life jacket. He tried and failed to get the other two out in time."

"Where's Walters?"

"Next door, zonked on morphine, just like you. He wasn't able to tell us much. We were hoping you might do better."

Stone told him what he could remember.

"Question," Leonard said. "Why were you all wearing life jackets? The standard ones were still stowed under the seats."

Stone explained about the ramp inspections at Teterboro.

"Well, I guess that FAA guy saved your life and Walters's, too."

"I guess so. Funny, Walters was there to protect the other two men, whose names were Roderick and Shepherd Troutman."

Leonard wrote down the names. "Protect them from what?"

"They had recently been involved in a business deal that went wrong, and threats were made against them. I guess I'll leave that for the FBI, or whoever conducts the criminal investigation."

"Fair enough. How long were you at your meeting in the FBO?"

"It was the Troutmans' meeting, not mine. I sat in the pilot's lounge and read a magazine article. About an hour and a half, I guess."

"Could you see the airplane from where you were sitting?"

"No, my back was to it. I was pointed at a big TV screen, which wasn't turned on."

"What was the magazine article about?"

"About a new autolanding system for King Airs and Pilatus PC-12s."

"I'm afraid your airplane was a total loss."

"I used to own the airplane, but I sold it to a company called Strategic Services, on whose board I serve."

"And who employs Karl Walters," Leonard said.

"That's right."

"Where were you headed when you took off?"

"Back to Teterboro. The Troutmans were headed to England tomorrow, aboard my G-500, but they had to depart from an international airport, and that's not the Vineyard."

"And where is that G-500 right now?"

"In the Strategic Services hangar at Jet Aviation, Teterboro. That's where the M2 was based, too."

"I think the criminal investigators are going to want to go over the G-500 with a fine-toothed comb."

"Fine by me."

"You'll be seeing more of me," Leonard said, then left the room.

The male nurse came in. "Can I borrow a phone?" Stone asked. "Mine got lost in the crash."

The young man laid one on his belly. "Dial nine for an outside line. Don't worry about the charges. They'll be on your bill."

"Did you find my wallet?" Stone asked.

He held up a plastic bag.

"You'll find my medical insurance card in there. Make sure that makes it into the system, will you?"

"Sure thing."

He dialed the number.

"Bacchetti."

"It's Stone."

A brief pause. "You're not dead?"

"I'm terribly sorry to disappoint you, but no."

"The report I read said four fatalities."

"Only two. The Troutmen didn't make it."

"You free for dinner tonight?"

"Not unless you like creamed chicken and Jell-O. Besides, I'm enjoying the morphine too much."

"I hear that's fun."

"More fun than the alternative."

"I'll make some calls, and try to find out if they're lying to you about your condition."

"I don't have a phone, but here's the number of the ER at the hospital on the Vineyard." He read it out. "Will you call Joan and tell her that all—well, nearly all—is well?"

"I'll call Lance Cabot, too. He's already been on the horn. Dinner tomorrow, maybe?"

"We'll see."

They both hung up.

FORTY-EIGHT

Stone woke early the following morning in an actual hospital bed, instead of on the slab in the ER. The male nurse came in with a tray bearing scrambled eggs, bacon, and toast. The nurse left and came back a few minutes later with a phone, which he plugged in, then handed to Stone. "Line three," he said.

Stone pressed line three. "Yes?"

"Stone, it's Mike Freeman. You okay?"

"Yep, and so is Karl Walters."

"Yeah, we talked. You're both getting out this morning, so I'm sending an airplane over for you at noon."

"Okay by me."

"How are you feeling?"

"Not bad. Ask me again after I've had my morning fix of morphine."

"There've been people all over your G-500 since yesterday, looking for bombs, I guess. We're putting it back together as fast as we can."

"No rush. The trip to England was for the Troutmen, and they're not going."

"Karl told me. He was very upset that he couldn't get them out of the Citation."

"I know how he feels. I'm not even sure how I got myself out."

"You must have done something right."

"I guess. I don't know who's talked to who, but if any crew shows up for the G-500 to England, send them home."

"That's all taken care of."

"Could you call Joan and ask her to send Fred to pick me up when I get there?"

"Sure."

"Thanks, Mike. I'm sorry about your airplane."

"We're already looking for a replacement. There are some out there."

"It's good to keep busy. Bye."

They both hung up.

The male nurse came in with the clothes Stone had worn the day before. "We washed and dried these, but we don't have an iron," he said, dumping them on the bed. "The doc will be in shortly."

———————

Dr. May Harris came in, poked at several sore spots on Stone's body, and gave him a nod. "I'll give you just one more shot of morphine, then you're out of here. A cab is coming for you and Walters at eleven." She emptied the syringe into his IV, wished him well, and left.

Karl Walters didn't want to talk much on the trip to the airport. He gave Stone the bare bones.

"I understand," Stone said. "I'm glad you got out."

"Me, too," he said.

When he got to the Strategic Service hangar they were still reassembling his G-500, and Fred was waiting. Soon they were at home.

"Welcome back to life," Joan said as he walked in.

"Thank you. Good to be back."

The phone rang. "That will be Dino," she said, going for it.

Stone sat down at his desk and picked up the phone. "Yeah?"

"It's Lance," the familiar voice said. "You're going to try to kill Gregor Kronk, aren't you?"

"Well, I'm not into actual murder, Lance, but I wouldn't pass up an opportunity to defend myself with lethal force."

"That's what I thought. For your information, Kronk was in Montreal all day yesterday, covering his tracks. Whoever planted the bomb was probably from the crew on his yacht, which is still anchored at Edgartown."

"I don't suppose you could lend me a couple of F-16s to blow it out of the water, could you?"

"Sorry, the F-16s are all booked up. You'll want to think about your next step very carefully. Kronk knows by now that you're still alive, so he'll be expecting you."

"Then I'll let him worry about that for a while, until I can think of something so diabolically clever that he won't see it coming."

"Whatever you think of, run it by me first, will you? I want to hang on to you, just as much as Kronk wants to kill you."

Stone made a laughing noise. "I'm so flattered that you feel that way, Lance."

"You just giggled. Let's talk again when the morphine wears off." Lance hung up.

Next call was really Dino. "Are you sober?"

"In a manner of speaking. I just talked to Lance, and he said I giggled."

Dino laughed aloud. "Caravaggio at seven?"

"Are we bringing women?"

"I am. I can't speak for you."

"See you then." Stone hung up and called Brooke.

"Your name was in the Vineyard paper," she said. "Phil called me."

"I'm happy to confirm their reporting."

"They reported you dead."

"In that case, I deny everything."

"Are Shep and Rod really gone?"

"They are, I'm sorry to say. There was a bomb on board our airplane. I was sitting at the opposite end from them, so I survived. So did their security guard."

"What happens now?"

"Whatever the universe is planning has been withheld from me. I know where I'm having dinner, though. Want to join the Bacchettis and me at Caravaggio at seven?"

"I'll meet you there, and I want to hear all the details."

"You'll have trouble stopping me."

"Where am I sleeping?"

"In my arms."

"Okay."

"But I'm just out of the hospital, so be gentle."

"Don't count on it." She hung up.

Joan was sitting across the desk from him. "All right," she said, "now I want all the details."

"I came, I saw, I flew, but not for very long."

"Not enough details."

"Somebody put a bomb in the airplane while I was waiting for Shep and Rod to meet with their architect, about rebuilding their properties on the Vineyard that got torched. It went off shortly after takeoff. I and their guard got out; they didn't. I don't know what else I can tell you."

"Your pupils look funny," Joan said.

"It's the morphine."

"It looks like you like it."

"Can you score me some more?"

Joan walked out, slamming the door behind her.

"I'll take that as a 'no,'" Stone said to nobody.

FORTY-NINE

Stone and Brooke arrived simultaneously at the door of Caravaggio and embraced warmly.

"I'm so glad to see you here," she said.

"I'm so glad to be here or anywhere else," he replied.

"Did you think you were going to die?"

"All I remember thinking about was staying alive. Let's go in, so I won't have to repeat myself."

Dino and Viv were parked at a real table, and they all embraced.

"I'm so glad I didn't see your death notice before Dino told me you were alive," Viv said, kissing him.

"I'm glad I didn't see it, either. I might have believed it."

"You must be hurting all over," Dino said.

"Morphine dealt with the worst of it," Stone said, "and bourbon is going to deal with the rest."

A waiter set that very thing down before him and inquired as to the ladies' pleasure. Then, all having been well-served, they peppered Stone with questions about his experience.

"What do you remember doing?" Dino asked.

"Two things: yanking the life jacket tight and turning the knob that released me from the seat and the harness. Everything else was just thrashing about."

"Where was the bomb?" Viv asked.

"In the tail section of the interior. Apparently, the rear luggage door was kept locked when not in use, so the bomb had to go in through the main cabin door and be tossed or placed aft. Some sort of altimeter must have set it off, and quickly. I never got the gear up. Fortunately I was unconscious soon after that. I woke up in the ER, and they said I had been out for five hours."

"I expect you needed the rest," Dino said.

"I still do," Stone replied.

"All right, all right, let's not milk it for all it's worth."

"I'm trying not to overstate the case. Morphine was my friend. Dino, do you think you could poke around your evidence locker and see if you can scare up some more of the stuff?"

"I could probably find you some crack and a dirty syringe," Dino said.

"Never mind."

They order dinner and another drink.

"Is the bourbon finding its way to all the right places?" Brooke asked.

"It's doing very nicely," Stone said, sipping from his second Knob Creek.

"So," Dino said. "How are we going to kill this guy?"

"Don't talk that way in front of Brooke. She'll get the wrong impression."

"I'm getting the right impression," Brooke replied. "And I want to help."

The others laughed.

"I just want to watch," Viv said. "Others can do the dirty work."

By the time they had dined, it was feeling like any other evening, Stone reflected. "It's nice to have friends who would have cared if the newspaper had been right," he said, raising a brandy glass to them all.

"It's nice to be drinking your cognac, instead of mine," Dino replied.

Brooke spoke up, "I think I had better get Stone home while he's still ambulatory."

"Yeah, and before he gets weepy," Dino said. "I don't think I could stand that."

The party broke up, and the celebrants went their ways.

I don't think I can undress myself," Stone said, sitting down heavily on the bed.

"I'll deal with that," Brooke said, working on his buttons.

"I wish I could do the same for you," he said, falling back onto the bed.

She got his feet under the covers and pulled them over him. "We'll finish this in the morning," she said, "when you're a new man."

"In the morning, I could have been dead," Stone said, then he fell soundly asleep.

"Poor baby," Brooke said, kissing him on the forehead and switching off the lights.

The following morning, with sunlight streaming through the blinds, Stones sat up, erect in every sense of the word.

"I see duty calls," Brooke said, pulling back the covers and mounting him.

"That was the patriotic response," Stone replied, doing what he could to help.

After they had collapsed and dozed off, they were awakened by the dumbwaiter's bell, and Brooke got up and served them.

"You look wonderful naked," Stone said, observing her sleepily.

"I'll bet you say that to all the girls."

"Only the naked ones."

"Shut up and eat breakfast," she said.

I t was mid-morning before Stone could bestir himself to dress, shave, shower, and go downstairs.

Joan brought him a sustaining second cup of coffee.

"Anything up?"

"A FedEx came from the lawyer in California, Ted Stein."

"Who?"

"From the L.A. office. He called about it. It's the closing documents on the Malibu house Shep bought, and some personal papers of his," she said. She left and came back with a FedEx box.

"Just leave it on the sofa," Stone said, opening the *Times*. "I'll go through it later." He began his morning stroll through the newspaper, and when that was done, settled into the crossword, with his feet on his desk and his chair rocked back.

J oan woke him in time for lunch. "Why are you so punchy this morning?" she asked. "Is this a hangover from the morphine?"

"If it is, it's very pleasant," Stone said.

The phone rang, and Joan answered it. "It's Lance," she said, covering the phone.

Stone picked up. "Good morning, Lance."

"You sound drowsy. Still on the morphine?"

"I haven't been able to get anybody to give me any."

"Careful, you may have an addictive personality," Lance said.

"If that were true, I'd have died from a diseased liver long ago."

"What a pleasant thought. Have you given any more thought to the Kronk problem?"

"I thought I'd let him sweat for a while, before I make a move."

"What move is that?"

"I haven't a clue," Stone said.

"You'd better come up with something before he does," Lance said, then hung up.

FIFTY

The next morning Stone sent Brooke home and went down to his office, feeling very much more sober than he had the day before. He actually got some work done before noon, when Joan buzzed. "It's that guy from the L.A. Woodman & Weld office, Ted Stein."

Stone picked up. "Good morning, Ted."

"You sound like a new man," Stein said.

"In a manner of speaking, I am."

"Did you have an opportunity to go through that package I sent you?"

"Not yet. I've been lazy."

"I think you're going to find it interesting, particularly the will."

"The will? Shep never mentioned a will."

"That's because he didn't have one. I suggested that before he bought the Malibu house might be a good time to address that, so he dictated a will, which required only a little editing, we typed it up for him and he signed, in the presence of enough witnesses to satisfy the states of both California and Massachusetts. I suggest you read it and call me back, if you have any questions. Oh, and after he signed the will he signed another document, making you his executor."

"Why two documents?"

"You'll see." Ted hung up.

Joan came in.

"Where's that FedEx box from Ted Stein?"

"It's in the Excelsior," she said.

"I hope to God you can open the beast," he said.

Joan disappeared into the back room and, after a few minutes, came back with the box. She set it on his desk, took a box cutter from her pocket, cut it open, and shoved it across his desk. "There you go," she said.

Stone upended the box, and everything spilled out on his desktop. The paperwork for the house seemed in order, as did the document naming him executor. Then he got to the will.

There was a fairly long list of schools, colleges, charities, and apparent friends, all of which or whom were left a million dollars each. He had forgotten how rich Shep had become before his death.

Then came the final bequest, which set him back on his heels.

The balance of my estate, whether in cash, securities, or real property, I leave and bequeath to my good friend and attorney, Stone Barrington, with all taxes to be paid by the estate.

Stone tried to make sense of that. How much did Charley Fox say Shep had deposited in his investment account? Stone believed he had said "two hundred and fifty million dollars." He sucked in a breath, then he remembered that he had deposited $150 million from Kronk into Shep's account two days before. He did some quick arithmetic on taxes and came up with a net of roughly $250 million. Then he remembered that there was the house in Lenox and those three newly leveled beachfront lots on Martha's Vineyard. Holy shit.

He called Ted Stein in L.A.

"I thought I'd be hearing from you," Ted said. "I take it you've read Mr. Troutman's will."

"I have."

"By the way, Shep's father left his entire estate to him. The documents are with Rod's personal attorney in Massachusetts. His card is in the envelope."

"Did you total the whole thing?"

"I think it's going to be in the neighborhood of four hundred million dollars, you poor guy. Not counting the real estate."

"Wasn't there some charity or school he'd rather have left it to?"

"Read the list, pal. They all got a mil each."

"Listen, Ted, I'm going to send all this stuff back to you and let you and our estate department handle it. I'm not going anywhere near it."

"Well, if you can hang on to it until tomorrow, I'll be in New York for the quarterly partners' meeting at Woodman & Weld. I'll go over it with the estate department and see what we have to do about probate. We probably ought to run it by the bar association, too."

"My secretary will deliver the whole package to you tomorrow," Stone said.

"I'll be using a temporary office in the Seagram Building."

Stone hung up and stuffed everything back into the FedEx box and gave it to Joan. "Reseal this and put it back in the Excelsior. Then tomorrow, please run it over to the offices and deliver it into the hot hands of Ted Stein, who'll be in a temporary office at Woodman & Weld."

"Will do," Joan said. "You look a little nauseated," she said. "Are you not getting enough morphine?"

"Please don't ever mention morphine to me again," he said.

"Touchy, touchy."

Stone stretched out on the leather sofa and closed his eyes.

FIFTY-ONE

Stone was late arriving for the partners' meeting at Woodman & Weld the following day, so he didn't have an opportunity to speak with Ted Stein, who was seated at the far end of the table.

When the meeting ended, Bill Eggers, the managing partner of the firm, who had presided, waved Stone into his office, next door to the conference room. Ted Stein joined them, too, and Peter Stern, the senior partner of the estates department, and a man Stone did not know, who was introduced as Edward Short of the New York Bar Association. A stenographer joined them, too.

Eggers spoke: "This is not a legal proceeding. The purpose of this meeting is to discuss the actions of our client, Shepherd Troutman, now deceased, when he called on Ted Stein in our

Los Angeles office on a matter concerning the purchase by Mr. Troutman of a house in Malibu Colony. We will also discuss the matter of Mr. Troutman's will. The meeting will be informal, and anyone may interrupt to ask questions at any time.

"Let's begin with Ted Stein of our Los Angeles office. Ted, did you have occasion to meet with our client, Shepherd Troutman, earlier this week? And if so, what was the purpose of this meeting?"

"I did," Stein replied. "Mr. Troutman was purchasing a house in Malibu Colony, and we met to close the sale."

"Did you close it?"

"Yes, we did."

"So, at the end of this meeting, Mr. Troutman was the legal owner of the house?"

"Yes, he was. I transferred the purchase price to the seller at the end of the meeting."

"Did you conduct any other business with Mr. Troutman?"

"Yes. I asked him if he had a will, and he responded that he did not. I suggested that he might make a will while he was in our office. He responded that he would, it was a good idea."

"What happened then?"

"A stenographer came in, and he gave her a list of a dozen or fifteen names, saying that he would like to leave each of those individuals or institutions one million dollars. Finally, when he was certain that the list was complete, he said that he would like to leave the remainder of his estate to Stone Barrington, his attorney in New York."

"Did he say why he had chosen Mr. Barrington for this honor?"

"He said that Mr. Barrington had been very helpful to him over the past weeks, to the extent of saving his life."

"Did he then conclude the will and sign it?"

"Yes." Stein took some papers from a FedEx box on the floor. "This is the original of the will."

Everybody was presented with a copy of the will.

"Was Mr. Barrington aware that such a will was being made?"

"No, Mr. Troutman told me that Mr. Barrington knew nothing of it. When I spoke to Mr. Barrington about the will later, he was surprised."

"Did Mr. Troutman also appoint Mr. Barrington executor?"

"Yes, in a separate document."

"When Mr. Troutman spoke, in his will, of the 'remainder' of his estate after bequests, did you have any idea of the extent of the 'remainder'?"

"I knew only of the Malibu house he had just purchased."

Eggers directed his attention to Stone. "Mr. Barrington, did you have any idea of the extent of Mr. Troutman's holdings?"

"I did. I knew that he had a large investment account with Triangle Investments and three vacant lots in Martha's Vineyard."

"What about the Lenox house?"

"I assumed that was in his father's name."

"Did Mr. Troutman and his father subsequently become deceased?"

"Yes, in an aircraft crash near the Vineyard airport."

"Who was the pilot of the aircraft?"

"I was."

"Were there other survivors?"

"Only one, a security guard, who was protecting Mr. Troutman."

"What was the cause of the crash?"

"A bomb had been placed in the rear area of the aircraft, and it exploded."

"And you knew nothing of the bomb?"

"Certainly not, or I would not have been piloting the aircraft."

"Mr. Barrington, do you have anything further to contribute?"

"Only that the elder Troutman told me that he had left everything to his son. I would be happy to answer any questions."

"Mr. Barrington," the bar association man asked, "were you aware that Mr. Troutman had made a will in your favor?"

"No, not until after his death, when Mr. Stein told me of it."

"Did Shepherd Troutman have any other family?"

"No, only his father."

"How do you know this?"

"The younger Mr. Troutman told me this directly, in one of our meetings."

"Did you suggest that Mr. Troutman make a will?"

"No, I assumed that a person of substance would have made a will as a matter of course."

"Thank you, Mr. Barrington." He addressed the meeting. "The bar association has no objection to the execution of this will."

Eggers looked around the table. "Does any other person here have any further information to impart regarding this will?"

The estates partner spoke, "We have no objection. It's a good will."

"Then this meeting is concluded."

Everybody got up and shuffled out.

"Congratulations," Eggers said to Stone.

"Oh, shut up, Bill," Stone said.

"Why are you so grumpy? I should think you'd be elated."

"Because I can't help feeling that at any moment, somebody is going to burst through the door and yell, 'Arrest that man!' Meaning me."

"Try and get over it. Our estates people will get the will through probate as soon as possible."

"Thanks, Bill, I appreciate you being helpful."

FIFTY-TWO

Stone got back to his office to find two phone messages waiting from him, from Lance Cabot and Dino. He called Lance first.

"Ah, there you are," Lance said.

"Where else would I be?"

"I was told you were at a partners' meeting at Woodman & Weld."

"I was."

"You sound a little down, Stone. What's wrong?"

"Lance, I have a feeling that you are the one with the bad news. What is it?"

"Well, Kronk is still alive, but then, so are you."

"I would already have killed him, if I thought I could get away with it."

"Is there something I can do to help?"

"You mean, send out an Agency assassination team and do away with Kronk?"

"I wouldn't put it in such naked terms."

"What would you clothe it in?"

"You might ask if there's anything I can do to keep Kronk from harming anyone else."

"Are we talking about me?"

"If you like."

"Lance, please don't order any hits on my behalf."

"You mean, you are going to do it yourself?"

"I wouldn't know how or where to find him, and if I did, I don't think I could walk up to him and put two in his head."

"That's unfortunate, because I know where he is."

"Where?"

"Aboard his yacht in Edgartown Harbor."

"I believe I requested F-16s to deal with that, and you declined."

"Don't be silly, Stone, I'm not going to blow up half a dozen innocent yachts in a crowded harbor, just to get at Kronk."

"If you were me, how would you go after him?"

"I have planners who deal with that sort of detail."

"Okay, how would they do it?"

Lance sighed deeply.

"I'm an amateur, Lance, I don't know how the pros accomplish this sort of thing. Give me some tips."

"You seem determined to make an accomplice of me."

"Actually, I do have an idea, but I'm going to need professional help."

"From what kind of profession?"

"Electronics and computer programming."

"I can help with that."

"I may call on you later," Stone said. "Let me give it some thought."

"As you wish," Lance said, then hung up.

Stone's phone rang immediately. "Hello?"

"It's Dino."

"Oh, hi."

"You sound desolate. What's wrong?"

"I just inherited nearly half a billion dollars that I don't deserve."

"Why do you think you don't deserve it?"

"I can't explain. It wouldn't make any sense."

"Tell you what, I'll take it off your hands and spend it gleefully. Would that help?"

"Not much." A green light on his phone began flashing. "I'll have to call you back." Stone hung up and pressed the button. "This is Stone Barrington."

"Will you accept a call from the president of the United States?"

"Yes."

"Hello, Stone?"

"Yes, Holly."

"I just heard about your flying accident. Are you all right?"

"It wasn't an accident, it was murder."

"Of whom? You're walking and talking, aren't you?"

"Of my client, Shepherd Troutman. He and his father were sitting in the back of the airplane when it exploded. They didn't survive."

"Oh, my God. You must feel awful."

"I do."

"You can't blame yourself for a murder committed by someone else."

"It turns out that I can."

"Oh, baby."

"There's an upside in this for you."

"How? What?"

"You remember the Malibu house?"

"Of course."

"My client bought it, then he made a will, leaving it to me, so I'm now the owner."

"But how . . ."

"I'm going to make you a two-pronged offer," Stone said. "If you decide not to run again, I'll give you the house. If you decide to run, I'll establish a political action committee and contribute ten million dollars to your campaign. You choose, at your leisure. I have to run now."

He then became one of the few people known to have hung up on a president. He called back Dino.

"Was that Holly?" Dino asked.

"Yes. Just between you and me, she told me when she was in L.A. that she is considering not running again. I went with her to look at a Malibu house."

"Did she buy it?"

"No, but Shep Troutman did. He left it to me."

"What are you going to do with a house in Malibu?"

"I offered it to Holly as a gift, should she decide not to run again."

"But not if she decides to run?"

"No, in that circumstance I offered her a ten-million-dollar campaign contribution."

"So you're not attempting to sway her either way?"

"That was my point."

"What would you really like her to do?"

"We talked about that while we were house hunting. She wasn't ready to make a decision."

"But you were."

"I made her my best offer, but she stalled me."

"Do you blame her? That's a tough decision."

"I don't blame her, I'm just trying to make it easy for her, either way."

"I think that was a good move."

"I hope so."

"So what are you going to do about Kronk?"

"I'm going to try to do what I told him I would."

"And what is that?"

"We'll talk about it when I see you. I'm not really sure it can be done."

"Dinner, Clarke's, six-thirty?"

"See you there."

They both hung up.

FIFTY-THREE

Stone was on his way uptown in the Bentley when his cell phone rang. "Yes?"

"Stone, it's Charley Fox. I'm glad you're alive to talk to."

"Thanks, Charley."

"Who's going to be in charge of Shep Troutman's account with us?"

"I am. He left a will. After a number of specific bequests, I'm his principal heir."

"Wow. Have his executor send me some paperwork, and I'll get the account transferred."

"I'm his executor."

"Well, I guess that's kosher. It happens sometimes that the executor and the heir are one and the same."

"The head of the estates department at Woodman & Weld and a guy from the bar association say that it's kosher."

"Great. Listen, I call with some news: Troutman Industries has filed an IPO. They're going public."

"We don't have any of that, do we?"

"No."

"Let's leave it that way. Take no action."

"Okay, we'll stay out of it. Kind of a pity, though. It's going be a sought-after stock. They just had a fabulous year."

"Good for them. Gotta run, Charley."

"Sure. See ya."

They both hung up.

Stone got out of the car at P. J. Clarke's and went inside. Dino was waiting at the bar, and so was his Knob Creek on the rocks. Stone took more than a sip.

"You're looking better," Dino said.

"I'm feeling better."

"Good news?"

"Could be. I'm not sure yet."

"So, what is it?"

"I'm not going to tell you, because I wouldn't want you to make an investment because of something I told you."

"Okay."

They were shown to their table and busied themselves with the menus. They ordered steaks, as usual.

"So," Dino said, "the Troutman company is going public?"

"How the hell did you know that?"

"I heard a rumor."

"Don't do anything about it, hear me?"

"Don't worry, I'm not going to mess with insider trading. What are you going to do?"

"I've already told Charley Fox not to touch it."

"I hear it's going to be a hot stock."

"I hope so."

Dino looked at Stone narrowly. "What are you up to?"

"Nothing, yet."

"I take it I don't want to know."

"Hang on a minute." Stone got out his phone.

"Who are you calling?"

"Herbie Fisher."

"Okay."

"Hello," Herbie said.

"Herb, it's Stone."

"Evening. I hear congratulations are in order."

"Thanks, but I have a question for you. Did Shep Troutman actually sell the apartment in the Carlyle?"

"No, that was a ruse, to keep those Russian guys away from it."

"So, it's in Shep's estate."

"It is, until the executor wants to do something with it. I hear that's you."

"Right. That's all I want to know, Herb. See you soon."

"What was that about?"

"Finish your dinner. We're going to commit burglary, sort of."

"Whatever you say," Dino replied.

After dinner they went back to Stone's house. He opened the Excelsior and removed a document, made some copies, and returned it to the safe.

Back in the Bentley, he said to Fred, "The Carlyle, please."

At the hotel, Stone went to the manager's office, but he had left for the day. He found an assistant manager.

"Good evening, Mr. Barrington. We were all very sorry to hear of Mr. Troutman's death."

"Thank you," Stone said, handing the man a copy of the document. "I'd like a key to the apartment."

"We sealed it on hearing of Mr. Troutman's death, but I'm happy to open it for his executor." He had a key card made and handed it to Stone. "This is a permanent card; it won't expire until you order it changed."

"Thank you," Stone said.

"Can we sit down and talk about this for a minute?" Dino asked. They found chairs in the lobby. "What are we about to do?" Dino asked.

"I told you, burglary. We did it once before, remember?"

"I remember, but I have a strong feeling that we'd better be able to successfully explain this to somebody at some point."

"Dino, I'm Shep's executor. I'm also his heir. I'm entitled to enter his property and do whatever I wish with the contents."

"What contents are we looking for?" Dino asked.

Stone explained what he wanted, though he wasn't entirely sure what it was.

"Okay, then. You're sure you don't want to take a tech with us?"

"Not unless we can't get into his safe. I saw Shep open it once, and I think I can remember the code. If I can't we'll need somebody with tools, who knows what do with them."

"Okay, I'm satisfied."

"Are you armed?"

"Does a gorilla have nuts?"

"Okay, just bear in mind that I'm not, and if we have any problems, try not to shoot me."

"Sometimes I want to shoot you," Dino said, "but you're in luck, not tonight."

They went in search of an elevator and found one without an operator. Stone inserted the key card, tapped in the floor number, and they started up.

They reached the floor, got off the elevator, and made their way to the front entrance of the apartment.

"Uh-oh," Dino said, pointing at the door.

Stone followed his finger. The door was just slightly ajar.

FIFTY-FOUR

Stone waved Dino away from the front door and down the hall a few feet. "I want to go in first," he whispered.

"So what's your plan? You're unarmed. You going to point your finger at him and say *bang*?"

"That's what I want."

"You want suicide by burglar?"

"We don't know he's armed."

"We don't know he's not, either. And in my book, armed is a safer bet."

"So what's *your* plan? You're going to shoot him on sight?"

"That's an option, if I can see him. On the other hand, I could blind him."

"Blind him how?"

Dino held up a tiny flashlight. "I once hit a guy with this beam, and he vomited."

"So you want to make him vomit?"

"Only as a distraction, until I can shoot him."

"He may have information we need."

"Like what?"

"Like the combination to the safe."

"You said you knew that."

"I said I *think* I know it."

"All right, why don't I wait for him to open it, then shoot him."

"That's an awful lot of paperwork."

"That's the first sensible thing you've said since we got here. All right, I'll just wing him."

"Wing him where?"

"In the wing? In the ass? Anywhere you like."

"It's going to be pitch dark in there," Stone said.

"We've got city lights in every window."

"Not if the blinds are closed."

"Okay, say it's pitch dark. What's your first move?"

"To let my eyes become accustomed to the darkness."

"You can do that right here, without getting shot."

"How?"

"Close your eyes for a minute, then ease in there, then open them."

"That could work," Stone said, closing his eyes.

"One more point before we go blundering in there," Dino said.

"What point?"

"The second we open the door he's going to see us, because of the light in the hallway."

"So you want to break all the light bulbs out here? That would be noisy."

"No, I want to turn off all the light switches. Look for some."

They found two light switches and turned them off. It got dark, but then the city lights at each end of the hallway came into play.

"I'll get the blind on this one," Stone said, pointing. "You get the other one."

They pulled the blinds, and it got very dark in the hall. "Okay," Stone said, "let's go."

"Okay."

"Me first."

"Not a chance; the guy with the pistol and the blindingly bright flashlight goes first, so shut up about it and stay behind me."

"Oh, all right," Stone said. "But one thing."

"Now what?"

"When you turn on the flashlight, don't blind *us*."

"I'll put my hand over it like this," Dino said, pressing a palm to the flashlight. "When we spot him, close your eyes."

"Okay, I can't think of anything else."

"Thank God for that. Let's go."

Dino felt along the wall with Stone's hand on his shoulder until he found the door. "Down," he said, crouching.

Stone crouched and kept a hand on Dino's back.

Dino eased the door open to reveal more blackness.

"Can you see him?" Stone whispered.

"I can't see a thing," Dino whispered back.

"What do we do now?"

Dino stood up, crept along the entrance hall until he found a group of four switches and turned them all on at once. The hall and living room lights came on, blinding them.

"Can you see anything?" Stone asked.

"Give it a minute."

"I can see a little." Dino held up his left arm, the flashlight in his fist and rested his shooting hand on his left wrist. He turned on the flashlight. "Do you see anybody?"

"No," Stone said. "Bedroom, straight ahead. That's where the safe is."

Dino walked across the living room and kicked open the bedroom door, playing his little flashlight around the room. "Nobody. Nothing."

"Let's have a look at the safe. It's in the closet, there."

Dino turned the doorknob and opened the closet door. As soon as it was open an inch, something heavy struck it, knocking both of them down.

"Man in black," Stone said, pointing toward the fleeing shadow across the living room.

"Come on!" Dino said, getting to his feet. There was no one in the living room, but the door to the hall was open. They heard a door slam and the sound of feet hitting steel stairs, getting farther away quickly.

"He's on the fire stairs." Stone tried to brush past Dino, but his arm was grabbed.

"Hold it," Dino said, "he's gone, and I'm not going to break my ass running down all those stairs."

"Elevator," Stone said. "Maybe we can beat him there."

They got back into the private elevator. Stone inserted the key card and pressed L. They began to descend quickly. "We've got a fighting chance," Stone said.

"Okay, you can go first," Dino said. "You tackle him and I'll cover you." He stood back to let Stone pass.

The elevator door opened, and Stone sprang out into an empty lobby.

"Which way did he go?" Dino asked.

"I've no idea. He could be in the street, or he could be ordering a drink in Bemelmans Bar. He could have a room booked upstairs somewhere."

"Well, shit," Dino said.

"Agreed."

"Let's go back and look at that safe," Dino said.

"Good idea."

"Only idea."

"Granted."

"This time, you can go first," Dino said, holstering his pistol and pocketing his flashlight.

Stone put the key card into the slot and entered the floor number. They began to rise.

FIFTY-FIVE

Stone let them back into the suite and led the way to the bedroom, where the door hung on a single hinge. "Give me your flashlight," he said to Dino.

Dino handed it over. "Don't blind yourself."

Stone played it around the closet. "Look, he left tools," he said, pushing a canvas bag with a toe.

"If we had argued another minute about who was going first, he might have gotten it open for us," Dino said. "Try the combination you think you remember."

Stone tried it, to no effect.

Stone squinted. "I can't remember it. I was thinking of my locker code at the YMCA."

"You belong to the YMCA?"

"I did, until I could have my own gym. I used that code every day."

"What was the code?"

"1-2-3-4."

"That was fiendishly clever of you," Dino said.

"Yeah, but my locker still got robbed. Check what's in the robber's bag."

Dino picked up the bag, turned it upside down, and emptied the contents onto the bed. "Hey," he said, picking up an officer's model 1911 Colt with thumb and forefinger, by the barrel. "You want me to shoot the safe?"

Stone looked through the stuff on the bed. There was a large ring of various kinds of keys, some small wrenches, a set of Allen keys, and a few other things. "I'm calling the manager." He got hold of the assistant manager who had given them the key card. "We need a locksmith up here, or a safe-cracker."

"I'll call somebody. They'll want more money for doing it at night. You want to wait until tomorrow?"

"No, right now, please."

Dino checked out the safe again. "It's bigger than most hotel safes," he said. "I think you could get a briefcase in there."

Stone looked at it. "I think so, too."

Dino went into the living room and switched on the TV. "We might as well be comfortable," he said, plopping down on the sofa and switching to Rachel Maddow. "That's one smart woman," he said.

"I agree."

"I'll bet she could open a hotel safe."

"I wouldn't put it past her."

Rachael was introducing Lawrence O'Donnell, who followed her, when the doorbell rang. Stone opened it and let in a man wearing coveralls with the name Al embroidered on the left chest. "You need help with your safe?"

"Right this way," Stone said.

"You have any ideas about the combination?"

"Well . . . you might try something that starts with 1-2-3-4," he said.

"That's clever! Familiar, too. You'd be surprised how many combinations start with those numerals."

"I'll wait in the living room," Stone said.

Lawrence was already interviewing his first guest.

"Mr. Barrington?" the tech called from the bedroom. "Can you come in here, please?"

Stone got up, went to the bedroom, and looked into the closet. The safe was open.

"What code did you use?" Dino asked from behind them.

"1-2-3-4-1-2," Al said. "That will be five hundred dollars."

"*What?*" Stone said.

"It would have been three hundred, if the sun was still up.

And that includes the drive from the Bronx. And putting in a new code. What code would you like?"

Stone gave him the last six digits of his Social Security number, then coughed up the cash. Al installed the new code and made to leave. "Any time," he said.

"Can you open an Excelsior?" Stone asked, apropos of nothing.

"An *Excelsior*?" Al asked. "You got one of those?"

"I do."

"Only one guy alive can open an Excelsior: his name is Sol Fink. Tell you what, I'll pay *you* five hundred to let me play with it for a day."

"As much as I'd like to entertain you, no," Stone said.

Al picked up his bag and left.

"Okay," Dino said. "What's in the safe?"

"I forgot to look," Stone said. He went to the safe and came back with an alligator briefcase, which he set on the bed and tried to open. It was locked.

"If we hurry, we can get Al back here for another five hundred," Dino said. He fiddled with the locks for a moment, then it opened.

"What was the combination?"

"Shep did what you would have done: it was 0-0-0."

Stone opened the case. There was a lot of cash, in ten-thousand-dollar bundles, a couple of pens, and a small book entitled *Coding for Security.* Stone opened it and flipped through it.

"What's that?" Dino asked.

"It's mostly a lot of zeros and ones," Stone replied. "I think it's just what we're looking for. All we need is somebody who can read it."

"Got any ideas?"

"Yeah. Huey Horowitz."

"Bingo!" Dino said.

Huey Horowitz was a computer whiz at the *New York Times* who had worked on a case with Stone. He was in his twenties and looked about fourteen. Stone called him.

"Huey, it's Stone Barrington."

"Stone! How are you?"

"Terrible. I need some help with computers and coding."

"It sounds boring," Huey said.

"It might be, to you. Can you come to dinner tomorrow night?"

"Describe your problem."

"It's an insoluble code."

"What time is dinner?"

"Six-thirty for seven."

"What does that mean?"

"Dinner's at seven. If you want a drink, show up at six-thirty."

"Can I bring a date?"

"Sure."

"See you at six-thirty." Huey hung up.

"What was that about?" Dino asked.

"Huey likes tough problems best, and he won't leave the *Times* before five o'clock. Bring Viv."

"We'd have to have dinner in Mumbai."

"Then come alone."

FIFTY-SIX

The following morning, Stone called Brooke.

"Hello, sailor."

"Are you up for a little dinner party tonight?"

"You betcha."

"Our guests will be a young man named Huey Horowitz, whose help I need, and his date, whoever that maybe."

"Can I bring anything?"

"Just your breasts, beautifully packaged and highly visible. Huey is susceptible to cleavage, and we want him happy."

"I never go anywhere without them. Is he inclined to unhappiness?"

"He's very, very bright, and it can be hard to get his full attention. If there are breasts in the room, it's easier."

"I'll do what I can," she said, then hung up.

Joan buzzed. "Mike Freeman on one."

Stone pressed the button. "Hi, Mike."

"I'm just wondering if you still need security people."

"More than ever, at least for a week or two," Stone replied.

"Something I should know about?"

"I'm supposed to be dead, and I'm not. Word is getting around."

"Any idea what form the threat will take?"

"Well, last time, it was a bomb. Do assassins like to repeat themselves?"

"They tend to have their specialties. The people who hire them don't."

"Then let's plan for everything. By the way, I'm having Dino and two outside guests over for dinner this evening, a young man and his girl, six-thirty."

"I can plan for that."

"I wouldn't want anything to happen to them."

"I understand, believe me."

Huey Horowitz stood still while his girlfriend, Trish, tied his necktie. He was okay with suits these days, but ties still defeated him.

"Who's this guy we're dining with?" Trish asked.

"A very interesting man named Stone Barrington. The food

and wine will be terrific—he has his own cook—and he's very good-looking."

"Will he have a date?"

"Absolutely, and if the past is any indication, she'll be a knockout."

"I like a little competition," Trish said, buttoning his collar and affixing his cuff links.

"You need a non-compete clause in your contract."

"We have a contract?"

"Well, I think so, but I'm not sure you do."

She laughed and kissed him. "You're sweet."

W ow," Stone said, when Brooke took off her coat.
"Well, you asked."

"And I have received in abundance."

"I'm not sure who this is for, Huey or you?" she said.

"It's a sight any male human being would be grateful for."
He heard Dino let himself in and call out.

They met him in the living room then went to the study.
Fred Flicker, Stone's man, stood by the bar.

"Wow," Dino said.

"Told you so," Stone said to Brooke.

Fred made their drinks, then stood by the front door.

"Who's Huey bringing?" Dino asked.

"We don't know."

"She's going to be jealous," he replied.

The bell rang, and a moment later, Fred appeared with Stone's guests. "Mr. Horowitz and Ms. Trish," he said.

"I'm Huey," he said to Brooke, his eyes widening slightly.

"And I'm just plain Trish," she said.

"She's a model," Huey said. "She doesn't have a last name."

"Not one that anybody could pronounce on the first try," Trish said.

Fred dealt with their drinks, brought a tray of canapés, then disappeared.

They chatted through drinks, then dined on foie gras, pheasant, and mille-feuille, a light cake, then had port and Stilton in the study.

O kay, Stone," Huey said. "What's your insoluble problem?"
Stone tossed him the book. Huey looked at it and smiled. "This is your insoluble problem?" he asked.

"Huey, as you well know, I am computer semiliterate, no more."

"I recall."

"Can you translate that material into something I can use?"

"Stone," Huey said, "I wrote this book."

"Eh?"

"It doesn't have my name on it, because my contract with the

Times says that they get first dibs, but this was a freelance job that wouldn't turn up in bookstores, and the money was fabulous."

"Who was your client?"

"I'm not supposed to say, but he's dead now, so what the hell? It was a man named Shepherd Troutman."

"Who was also my client, and whose executor I am. Do you know how he died?"

"Something about an aircraft accident."

"I was flying the aircraft, and it wasn't an accident, it was a bomb."

Huey blinked. "Oh."

"He was murdered by—or on the instructions of—a man named Gregor Kronk, who bought the family business from the Troutmans but neglected to buy the patent rights to a lot of crucial equipment, in each of the seven plants, worldwide."

"I know about the patent rights. That was what this book addresses. What's the problem now?"

"Once, in earnest conversation with Kronk, I made a threat that if he harmed the Troutmans we would reduce his factories to smoking ruins, by manipulating the machines' software. Now that Kronk has murdered both of them, I don't know if I can actually do that. Can you?"

"I can make the machines run backward, if I want to," Huey replied.

"Huey, I believe we're getting somewhere," Stone said.

FIFTY-SEVEN

S tone was feeling better now, and an occasional glance at
Brooke's bosom was holding Huey's attention.

"Here's the important thing," Stone said. "Can you
teach me to do it at will? There will come a moment when I
want to do it, but I can't control when that will be, and you will
not be available 24/7, right?"

"Absolutely, unalterably right," Huey said. "Fortunately,
you are not the first to need these skills." He took hold of his
book, held it by the spine and shook it. A folded sheet of paper
fell from it and landed on the coffee table.

"What is that?" Stone asked.

"Instructions for idiots," Huey replied.

"You've got the right man."

"Fortunately, Shep Troutman was only slightly more

semiliterate with computers than you. So, through repetition and following these instructions, he was able to control the software at will." He unfolded the sheet of paper and handed it to Stone.

Stone found himself confronted with a page of ones, zeros, and various other gobbledygook. "I think I'd have to learn to read all over again," he said.

"Do you have a computer at hand?" Huey asked.

"Downstairs in my office. Ladies, Dino, if you will all excuse us. We should be done by next Tuesday."

"It won't take as long as that," Huey said, following Stone downstairs.

Stone switched on the lights and turned on the computer. "I hope this will do," he said, "because it's all I've got."

"Let's see," Huey said, sitting down and letting his fingers fly around the keyboard. Various code and computer imagery bounced around the screen. Finally, he stopped.

"Is that it?"

"If you're Bill Gates, yes. Unfortunately, you are you and require further instruction. I'll make this as simple as I can: I taught Shep to operate the software that controlled the machines. He could turn them on and off, vary their performance, change the times and dates for auto-programming, after checking to see that the rental fees had been received, then turn them off if the fees had not been paid."

"That's a lot."

"It is for you. My question is: Exactly what do you want the machines to do? If you can explain that to me, I can write a little program that, when activated, will do that and nothing else. Or, perhaps, give you an option or two."

"I would like to be able to turn the machines on and off, just to demonstrate to Kronk that I can do it, then I'd like an option that will cause the machines to, in effect, commit suicide."

Huey laughed aloud. "I've never been asked to make a machine take its own life," he said. "That's intriguing."

Stone was happy to have something that could hold Huey's interest, besides Brooke's breasts. "Make it really, really simple," he said.

"Can you type a single word, then hit enter?" Huey asked.

"Probably," Stone said.

"All right, what I'll do is write three programs. Give me three words."

"Apple, Orange, Avacado."

"Good. I'll write a program that 'Apple' will turn on, 'Orange' will turn off, and 'Avocado' will turn the machinery into, effectively, guacamole."

Stone laughed. "I like it."

Huey typed fleetly for, perhaps, six or seven minutes. "Oh, and let's give the program a one-word name." He looked at Stone and waited.

"Cleavage," Stone said.

"Perfect. Remember, all caps."

"Right, all caps."

"Now, let's start from the beginning." He shut down the

computer and switched it off, then on again. "Here's your start-ing page," he said, when the machine had booted up. An empty box appeared on the screen. Huey typed in CLEAVAGE, and hit enter. Another page appeared, with the words, APPLE, ORANGE, and AVOCADO, each with an empty box next to it. "All you do is check the box you want. I could demonstrate, but since these factories are scattered about the world, we'd probably shut down something, somewhere, that someone is operating, and they'd start calling for help. They might get it, and we don't want that."

"Right."

Huey did some more typing. "I've added an option on the title page," he said. "It's called 'Time Bomb,' and it has boxes for hours, minutes, and seconds. You fill in date, time, etcetera, up to twenty-four hours, then start the program as usual. When the time is up, *voilà*! You've got yourself lots of guacamole!"

"I like it," Stone said.

Huey printed half a dozen copies of the page and instruc-tions and gave them to Stone. "In case you lose five of them."

"And I can do this from any computer?"

"Any PC. You want me to write you another version for an Apple?"

"No, don't bother. We have only PCs in the office."

"Then we're done."

"Listen, Huey, you may hear around your office that Trout-man is going public. It would be a terrible mistake to either buy or sell the stock, or to tell someone who might do so. Insider trading is a great big NO-NO. Do you understand?"

"Of course."

"Not even Trish."

"No? Well, all right, though it would certainly impress her if I could make her a quick fortune."

"You'd have to look at her breasts through prison bars, when she came to visit."

"I'll restrain myself," Huey said.

They went back upstairs and rejoined the others.

"Get it all done?" Dino asked.

"Huey did. I'll explain it all later."

"By the way," Huey said, "if you start the program from outside your local area network, you'll have to type in the function you're selecting, not just check a box."

Stone wrote that instruction on the cheat sheet Huey had provided. "Got it."

"Are you going to monkey with their machinery now?" Dino asked.

"No, I'm going to wait until they go public," Stone replied. "They'll announce the date soon, and I'll confirm it with Charley Fox."

"Can I watch?"

"Maybe. We'll see."

FIFTY-EIGHT

Friday morning Stone was at his desk when Joan buzzed him.

"There's a man on the phone who says that he's your architect," she said.

"I don't have an architect," Stone replied.

"Hang on." She put him on hold for a few seconds, then came back. "He's a Mr. Whitman of Whitman & Whitman in Edgartown, Massachusetts."

"Ah, got it." He pressed the button. "Mr. Whitman?"

"Yes, Mr. Barrington. I'm the second Whitman in our firm title, Ben. Twenty-five years ago, my father, Raymond, designed the three houses that were built for Rod Troutman, and his son, Shepherd. After they burned Shep had asked me to rebuild the three houses."

"I see."

"We're now ready to begin reconstruction, and we've engaged the original builders to do the work. However, with the demise of the Troutmans, I'm without a client to give final approval, and I'm told that you are Shep's executor and are authorized to do so."

"That's correct. I'm also Shep's heir."

"I wonder if it would be possible for you to pop up to the Vineyard for a couple of hours, to go over a few points with us. I don't want to get it wrong, then have to start over."

"When?"

"Monday, any time, would be good."

Stone thought about it. "Yes, I can do that."

"Lovely. We're in Edgartown." He gave Stone the address.

"Oh, Ben, a question for you. What sort of computers do you have in your office?"

"Apples."

"Do you have a PC in your office?"

"Yes, my secretary has both."

"Good. I'll see you around two on Monday afternoon."

"That's perfect."

They exchanged cell numbers, then hung up.

Stone called Mike Freeman and made arrangements to borrow another of his aircraft, a JetProp, a single-engine turboprop once owned by Stone, for the round-trip flight. He checked the five-day forecast, which promised fine weather for the trip.

L ater in the day, Joan buzzed him again. "You won't believe this, but Gregor Kronk is on the phone."

"Record the call, then make some noises like a long-distance connection and put him on." Stone waited a few seconds, then picked up the phone. "Yes?"

"Ah, Mr. Barrington, I'm glad to have caught you in New York."

"I'm not in New York, I'm abroad. My secretary connected us." First step, pretend to be somewhere else.

"No matter. In the interest of making peace between us, I wanted to give you a useful and profitable piece of news: Trout-man Industries is making a public offering on Monday, and since you are cash rich these days I thought I would give you an opportunity to make another fortune in a day. The stock is selling at eleven dollars a share, and after the initial public offering, it could go to a hundred, perhaps even two hundred dollars a share within a short time."

"I have not the slightest interest in profiting from anything to do with you or your company," Stone said, "and beyond that I do not deal with people who murder my friends and clients and attempt to murder me."

"Mr. Barrington, I hope you do not think that I was behind that."

"I certainly do think that, and I would not believe for a moment that you were innocent of it. You are a vile human being,

Mr. Kronk, and I will not speak to you nor listen to you for a moment ever again." Stone hung up with a feeling of some satisfaction.

Stone called Charley Fox. "Charley, have you had any communication from me the past couple of days?"

"Well, yes, I received your e-mail, instructing me to buy ten thousand shares of Troutman Industries."

"Have you done so, yet?"

"I was about to."

"The e-mail wasn't from me; Kronk sent it. He's trying to connect me to his IPO and frame me for insider trading, and I won't have it. Respond to the e-mail saying that I have given no such instruction, nor will you accept such."

"I'll do it immediately."

"Thank you, Charley."

"You and I should get together soon to discuss what you want to do with your inheritance."

"After probate. Bye, Charley." He hung up.

Stone called Dino.

"Bacchetti."

"It's Stone. Feeling like some lobster? Would you like to fly up to the Vineyard with me for lunch on Monday?"

"There are some words in that invitation that puzzle me," Dino said.

"What are they?"

"'Vineyard,' and 'fly.'"

"Coming over all queasy, are we?"

"Stone, I know you have a short memory at times, but try and remember what happened the last time those words appeared in the same sentence."

"I'm taking precautions."

"Precautions like having the New York City police commissioner in the airplane with you, in the hope that Kronk and his people will be put off by that?"

"That's one of them. I'll also have a security man stay with the airplane the whole time we're there, to be sure that no one loads a little extra cargo in it."

"Go on."

"And you'll get to see the plans for the new house you're going to buy on the Vineyard."

"Why should I buy a country house when you've got them all over the place, fully staffed and ready to feed me?"

"You have a point. Are you coming with me on Monday?"

"What time?"

"Pick me up at my house at nine AM. You'll be back in time for your first drink of the day. Oh, and we'll be flying in my old JetProp, which Kronk doesn't even know about."

"See you then." Dino hung up.

Stone called Mike Freeman.

"Yes, Stone?"

"I'd like to have a man to stay with the airplane at the Vineyard airport to be sure nobody stashes a bomb in it."

"I've got a couple of men camping out on the burned-out property to keep it safe. I'll have one meet you and stay with the JetProp."

"Thank you, Mike."

"The boys at Teterboro will give it a complete going-over to be sure it's not carrying any unnecessary baggage."

"I'd appreciate that, Mike." They both hung up. Stone was already feeling a little queasy, and it was only Friday.

FIFTY-NINE

Gregor Kronk sat in the conference room of the Wall Street firm handling the initial public offering of Troutman Industries, staring at a huge monitor screen.

"We're an hour and a half in, and we're up 140 points," an executive said. "It's going very well, and projections are telling us it will go higher, perhaps much higher."

Kronk sat and beamed. He was growing richer by the minute.

Stone and Dino presented themselves at the reception desk of Whitman & Whitman. A young man in shirtsleeves appeared and shook their hands. "I'm Ben Whitman. Come with me, please."

Stone and Dino followed him into a large conference room. Taking up most of the big table was an architect's model of what appeared to be a resort, which included cottages, a beach, and a marina.

"This," Ben said, "is what Shep Troutman came to see and approved on the day he died."

"I see the three houses that are being rebuilt," Stone said, "but I see a lot more. What is all this?"

"It's what was going to be called Troutman Bay, but at our meeting Shep had informed me he planned to discuss with you the possibility of bringing it under the Arrington Brand. He thought you might like the name 'The Vineyard Arrington.'

"I can see why you might feel a little stunned," Ben continued. "Shep and Rod recently spent some time at your Bel-Air Arrington, in Los Angeles, and they were very impressed with your execution of the place and the feel of it. The main house is pretty much as it was. The central house has been turned into a reception center, restaurant, bar, etcetera, and the third house is the yacht club."

"The whole thing is spectacular," Stone said, "but how would you ever get planning permission from the local authorities?"

"First of all, this land has been held in a Troutman family

trust for nearly a hundred years, and because of that they're working under a different set of planning rules. Secondly, as you can see, all the buildings are shingle-style. When it's done, you will think that the property has been around for a century. It blends beautifully with the landscape. Viewed from the water, it's even better, and the only new structures are the cottages, twenty-five of them."

Stone saw a large TV set on a wall. "Could you turn that on, please, and tune it to CNBC? There's something going on I want to follow." He watched as the TV came on. Immediately, someone was talking about the Troutman IPO and how fast the stock was moving up.

"What's wrong?" Dino asked.

"Ben, you said your secretary has a PC. May I use it for a few minutes?"

"Sure."

"I won't keep you long." Stone followed him to the computer, and while it booted up, he called Huey Horowitz.

"Yeah?"

"Huey, it's Stone. The IPO started at nine-thirty this morning, and I set the program for that time, but nothing has happened."

"Tell me how you set it up," Huey said.

Stone went through the procedure he had used. "I followed your cheat sheet."

"Let me take a look at it." Stone could hear the clicking of computer keys. "I think I've found the problem. Spell the word avocado for me."

"A-V-A-C-A-D-O."

"There's your problem," Huey said.

"Where?"

"The correct spelling is A-V-O-C-A-D-O."

"Oh, shit."

"Well, yes. What time did you set it for?"

"Nine-thirty AM."

"Then let's reset it. Pick another time."

Stone looked at a clock on the wall. It was 11:50 AM. "Twelve noon," he said, looking at the computer before him. "It looks correct now."

"All you have to do now is wait for noon."

"Thank you, Huey. I'm sorry to have been so stupid." They both hung up, and Stone went back to the conference room.

"Everything all right?"

"Just fine."

"Please tell me what you think of all this?"

Stone looked at the model. "How soon can you start?"

"About two and a half hours ago, on the main house," Ben replied.

"Then don't stop until it's finished. I'd like you to photograph the model and send it, will the specifications, to a list of my associates, which will be provided shortly by my secretary." He made the call to Joan, then called Marcel DuBois in Paris, then Mike Freeman and Charley Fox in New York. He held a hand over the phone. "How much do you want right now?"

Ben told him.

"Charley, did you hear that? Then wire the funds from my account to Whitman & Whitman in Martha's Vineyard. Here, Ben Whitman will give you wiring instructions." He handed Ben the phone, then he walked around the model again.

Ben gave him a DVD disk. "Take this home with you and see if you have any other questions."

Stone sat down and took a deep breath.

Kronk and his associates were in the middle of lunch when the first call came. He left the table and took the call. "Yes?"

"Mr. Kronk, this is the Lenox office. Something has gone wrong with the machinery."

"What?"

"First, the multilathe went down, then half a dozen other machines. We can't restart any of them. It's like before when Shepherd Troutman screwed them up. Hang on, I've got a call coming in from Mumbai."

A secretary came in. "Mr. Kronk," she said, "I have calls coming in for you from England, Kenya, and Brazil. They all say it's very urgent."

"Put them on hold." He went back to the Lenox call. "It's Kronk. What's happening now?"

"Everything has shut down. Every plant."

"Well, get them restarted before the market hears about this!"

"We're doing our best, sir."

Kronk hung up, and every member of his party were standing, staring at him. One of them was holding a phone.

"What have you done?" the man with the phone asked. "You told us this problem was permanently resolved."

"Please be patient," Kronk said. "We'll sort it out."

"Start selling," the man said, and people ran for their desks.

A half hour later, the world knew. Kronk was sitting on a sofa with a large Scotch in his hand, sweating.

S tone and Dino had lunch at the firm, then headed back to the airport. They had just turned in their rental car and were walking out to the airplane when Dino's phone rang.

The man charged with guarding the JetProp shook Stone's hand. "No one has approached the airplane for any reason," he said.

Stone got into the cockpit and ran through the checklist, while he waited for Dino to finish his call. A couple of minutes later Dino sat down and began buckling in.

"Anything important?" Stone asked.

"Sort of. We answered a 911 call from a Wall Street investment bank: an apparent suicide, but my people think it was probably staged."

"Who?"

Dino smiled a little. "Kronk," he said.

AUTHOR'S NOTE

I am happy to hear from readers, but you should know that if you write to me in care of my publisher, three to six months will pass before I receive your letter, and when it finally arrives, it will be one among many, and I will not be able to reply.

However, if you have access to the Internet, you may visit my website at www.stuartwoods.com, where there is a button for sending me e-mail. So far, I have been able to reply to all my e-mail, and I will continue to try to do so.

If you send me an e-mail and do not receive a reply, it is probably because you are among an alarming number of people who have entered their e-mail address incorrectly in their mail software. I have many of my replies returned as undeliverable.

Remember: e-mail, reply; snail mail, no reply.

When you e-mail, please do not send attachments, as I never

open these. They can take twenty minutes to download, and they often contain viruses.

Please do not place me on your mailing lists for funny stories, prayers, political causes, charitable fund-raising, petitions, or sentimental claptrap. I get enough of that from people I already know. Generally speaking, when I get e-mail addressed to a large number of people, I immediately delete it without reading it.

Please do not send me your ideas for a book, as I have a policy of writing only what I myself invent. If you send me story ideas, I will immediately delete them without reading them. If you have a good idea for a book, write it yourself, but I will not be able to advise you on how to get it published. Buy a copy of *Writer's Market* at any bookstore; that will tell you how.

Anyone with a request concerning events or appearances may e-mail it to me or send it to: Putnam Publicity, Penguin Random House LLC, 1745 Broadway, New York, NY 10019.

Those ambitious folk who wish to buy film, dramatic, or television rights to my books should contact Matthew Snyder, Creative Artists Agency, 2000 Avenue of the Stars, Los Angeles, CA 90067.

Those who wish to make offers for rights of a literary nature should contact Anne Sibbald, Janklow & Nesbit, 285 Madison Avenue, 21st Floor, New York, NY 10017. (Note: This is not an invitation for you to send her your manuscript or to solicit her to be your agent.)

If you want to know if I will be signing books in your city, please visit my website, www.stuartwoods.com, where the tour schedule will be published a month or so in advance. If you wish me to do a book signing in your locality, ask your favorite bookseller to contact his Penguin representative or the Penguin publicity department with the request.

If you find typographical or editorial errors in my book and feel an irresistible urge to tell someone, please write to Patricja Okuniewska at Penguin's address above. Do not e-mail your discoveries to me, as I will already have learned about them from others.

A list of my published works appears in the front of this book and on my website. All the novels are still in print in paperback and can be found at or ordered from any bookstore. If you wish to obtain hardcover copies of earlier novels or of the two nonfiction books, a good used-book store or one of the online bookstores can help you find them. Otherwise, you will have to go to a great many garage sales.